HENRY FICKLE
AND THE SECRET LABORATORY

BY
MICHELE MACK

ILLUSTRATIONS BY JAMES BROWNE

THE SORCERER'S PRESS

FOR THE CHILD IN US ALL

Library of Congress Catalog Card Number: 2003098600

ISBN: 0-9667747-1-X

10 9 8 7 6 5 4 3 2 1
Printed in the U.S.A.
First edition, 2004

Jacket art by James Browne
Jacket design and interior design by Lightbourne, Inc.

CONTENTS

HENRY FICKLE

AND THE SECRET LABORATORY

CHAPTER ONE

THE UNINVITED GUESTS

Willow Creek was a quiet town, the kind everyone called "an old fashioned sort of place." Nothing new or unusual ever happened. In fact, it was a most boring and unhappening place to be.

When you'd pass by the worn and rusted sign that read, "Welcome to Willow Creek, Established 1714, Population 1,614," you could have held your breath from one end of town to the other. That's how small it was. Everyone knew each other, especially when juicy gossip was going around, like the time George McNulty, the town's gardener, had coffee at Betty Lou's Kitchen with Mrs. Peachtree, who just happened to be on her third marriage.

The town had a scanty police department, one-garage firehouse, and the *Willow Times*, which was the most uneventful newspaper ever printed, until something unthinkable happened.

Avid readers woke up to a large photograph of the wrinkly face of Henry Fickle, with his scruffy beard and messy gray hair, across the front page. The bold headline read:

BREAKING NEWS

Henry Fickle is reported missing, the police announced late last night. "The case is under investigation," said the chief of police, Smitty, standing outside the station. "If anyone has any information, you're advised to contact our office immediately." Smitty declined to answer any more questions, except to confirm no evidence was found of a break-in and no suspect was taken into custody, as of today.

Fickle's sudden disappearance had been discussed so many times that nobody was quite certain what the truth was anymore. Everyone's interpretation of the tale, however, started in a similar way: Ralph Picit, the mailman, had delivered a large package to Fickle's house, and nobody had seen or heard of Fickle since. He had vanished mysteriously, leaving no trace of what happened. Had he been kidnapped or, worse yet, *murdered?*

Over at the Watering Hole, the town tavern, the gossip circulating was that Fickle supposedly had a laboratory in his house. "Always thought Henry was a nut," George McNulty told the eagerly listening folks, after his third shot of whiskey. "He went crazy in the head, he did."

"I quite agree," said a toothless man sitting at the bar. "Why would he be wanting a laboratory?"

The two men exchanged tense looks.

"He had a mad look about him, if you ask me," said an older woman, sipping her wine. "Never associated with anyone. Kept his business to himself . . ."

"Ah, terrible childhood," said the bartender, shaking his head. "I remember my grandfather telling me, when Henry was just ten-years old . . ."

Nearly a year had passed since Willow Creek had awakened to the shocking news about Henry Fickle, but nothing changed. Nobody had seen any suspicious strangers, and since Fickle's body was never found, the police were convinced the old man had skipped town.

Worn and ripped newspaper clippings dangling from store bulletin boards really showed how Fickle had become old news. Folks moved on with their lives and became interested in other matters. The *Willow Times* had been busy announcing that Dr. Rufeous Hearty's retirement party would be held at the local fire company. And, of course, there was the annual bake sale and craft show.

Some curious folks still ventured past the rickety house, even though it had been a year since Henry Fickle lived there. It stood perched alone on a hill at the end of Windy Drive. Folks felt the old house was creepy, and kids often threw stones through the windows. Once a worthy-looking structure with its massive iron gates, the house was now deteriorated and abandoned.

Since Fickle never married or had any living relatives to take over his humble possessions, his belongings were given to charity and the house put up for sale, although no bids were offered.

Then, just when things were back to normal, the Allbrights moved into town, which changed everything. The case of Henry Fickle had been kept secret from outsiders, and for a very good reason. If word leaked out, if others found out a murder may have been committed—well, Willow Creek's name would be scarred forever. When the gossip about the Allbrights reached every ear our story starts.

Dr. Allbright was a tall man with flaming red hair. His eyes were like tiny buttons behind his thick glasses. Dr. Allbright needed a change and was determined to make a new start for his family. He'd grown tired of the glamorous city life and dreamed of settling in a small town. After spontaneously using a vacation day, Dr. Allbright drove off alone and headed in a new direction. By some strange luck, and many back roads later, his car found Willow Creek.

Dr. Allbright spotted Dr. Hearty's retirement posted in the *Willow Times*. Since there were no qualified applicants applying for the vacant position, the town had no choice but to offer Dr. Allbright the job. Dr. Allbright was so happy he called his wife and told her to pack her bags.

Dr. Allbright immediately fell in love with Fickle's house, even though Harriet Wimple, Willow Creek's real estate agent, tried to tell him it was unsafe and possibly haunted. (Wimple swore she'd seen a pearly-white figure glide past an upper round window.) Not believing in such nonsense, Dr. Allbright persisted, even though the house needed some work. Windows were broken, the roof leaked, and the lawn looked like it hadn't been mowed in years.

Mrs. Allbright was thin with a long neck. Her blond hair was shaped into a tight bun, which was held firmly in place with a flowery clip. She would be the new science teacher at Willow Creek Elementary—her fact-finding profession taught her to ignore anything beyond science.

The Allbrights had two children. Dillon resembled his father, skinny and freckle faced with a head of red hair. He had trouble keeping his big-framed glasses over his bright blue eyes. They kept slipping down his long nose. He was an ambitious ten-year-old, and his parents often found him in the garage tinkering with odd inventions. One time he didn't eat for a whole day because he was obsessed with finishing a project.

Sarina was a shy, petite eight-year-old with cascading blond hair like her mother's. She followed Dillon everywhere, especially when he was building something astonishing. Sarina thought Dillon was a genius, his parents thought he was erratic, and others thought he was from another planet.

It was late August and nearly midafternoon when the town's nosiest neighbors peered through their curtains, watching the moving van make a wide turn onto Windy Drive. The muffler spit out a loud bang as it crawled its way toward the top of the hill. The atmosphere on the streets of Willow Creek was extremely tense. Uninvited guests made the folks uneasy and restless.

Kipper Reeves, the newspaper boy, skidded his bike just short of the Fickle house's spiked iron gate. He sat there open-mouthed watching the van drive up the long gravel drive. He couldn't believe someone had actually bought Fickle's house. They must have been fearless of Fickle's ghost.

On top of the pillars sat towering statues with intense-looking eyes. To the left of Kipper was an Egyptian god with the words "Thoth, keeper of the records" carved into the stone. On the right was an Egyptian goddess with huge wings. The words "Isis, goddess of the underworld" were carved at her feet. Kipper had never seen such serious statues—statues that looked to be guarding something very important.

A strong gale made the tree branches curtsey along the gravel drive. Dillon Allbright had been watching the tall, lanky boy from the rear window of the family car. He turned in his seat and smiled, knowing they'd be best friends before the day's end, knowing he'd meet two other kids, whose last name started with the letter *F*, and knowing that he had unique abilities. But he couldn't foresee that at this very moment, two people meeting in secret knew he'd arrived and were saying in excited voices, "Dillon Allbright is here at last!"

CHAPTER TWO

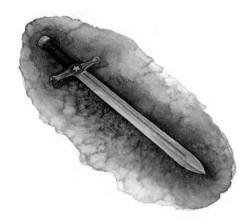

THE GHOSTS AND THE SWORDS

Dillon and Sarina clambered up a flight of stone steps. An overgrowth of unmanicured ivy crept around an arched oaken door. Two gloomy windows stood to each side, staring like a pair of eyes, as if they were waiting for company.

Something caught their attention, something unusual.

A ragged chair on the porch happened to be rocking by itself.

Goosebumps traveled up and down Dillon's spine. He stared—and saw, quite clearly, an elderly man sitting in the chair, rummaging through a large package. Dillon was about to ask what he was doing, when the man lifted the box, stood up, and turned. He ambled slowly toward a stone wall. He was almost there, and then, suddenly, he vanished.

Dillon turned quickly around and said, "Whoa—did you see that?"

Sarina Allbright didn't answer. Although she couldn't see the old man, seeing the moving, bodiless chair gave her an impression of what was ahead. She stepped backward, looking like she wanted to run, but was frozen with fear. Before she could say anything, Dillon reached for the doorknob.

The heavy door creaked open before he touched the knob. Maybe it's the wind, he thought.

They found themselves in a two-story, stone foyer; a wooden staircase facing them led to the bedrooms. The only sound they heard was the voice of their mother telling the moving men how to unload an expensive china cabinet. They weren't sure which room to explore first, until a hanging chandelier at the top of the stairs flickered.

Dillon and Sarina looked at each other with raised eyebrows. They'd heard haunted houses existed, but had never been in one. They trudged up the steps, trying not to make a sound, when Dillon stepped on a loose board. They froze, listening to the split of the wood crackle through the empty house. If the house had been sleeping, now they were sure it was awake. They climbed carefully onward.

At the top of the staircase was a long hallway with a row of closed doors to each side. Picture hooks were left on the walls where portraits must have hung. Although the hall was empty, Dillon sensed someone there, but before he could say anything—

THUMP! THUMP!

He heard heavy footsteps at the other end of the hall. The blood drained from his face as he stared into the emptiness. If his sister met a ghost—a real ghost—she'd faint before she got introduced.

CLINK! CLINK!

There was the sound of swords clashing, then another set of footsteps. It sounded like two men fighting a duel, but the hall was empty. Dillon looked around anxiously and saw nothing but his sister's calm face.

"What's wrong?" Sarina asked at once, taking a step backward. "Did you *see* something?"

"Er . . . no," mumbled Dillon. "You didn't hear anything, did you?"

As he expected, Sarina looked confused. After all, she'd never understood his unique abilities.

"No," she said nervously. "Why?"

"It was nothing," Dillon muttered, pretending to take interest in an antique fixture, but Sarina didn't buy it.

At a very early age, Dillon had been capable of penetrating the thin veil separating the physical and spiritual worlds. Dillon Allbright was clairvoyant and could see spirits. In his mind's eye, he'd see words, objects, symbols, and colorful scenes. He was also clairaudient and clairsentient. With his psychic ear, he'd hear sounds, voices, and tones beyond normal hearing range. And if a spirit was in the room, he'd sense its presence.

Dillon felt frustrated because no one ever understood his visions. So he drew a "psychic chart" in his notebook and recorded the repeated images. For instance, white roses usually meant a celebration like a birthday or a marriage, while an eerie coffin meant someone was going to die. At times, the images were so vivid, they'd appear real.

The dueling ghosts hadn't revealed themselves; however, the clanging and straining grunts told him they were getting closer and closer. Dillon took a step backward. What was happening? It was as if a parallel world existed in the same space.

The front door suddenly swung open. Two muscular men stepped inside carrying the heavy china cabinet. The sword fight stopped at once, leaving only the voice of Mrs. Allbright, directing the men through the rooms.

Dillon cast one last, terrified look at the silenced hallway and grabbed Sarina's hand. Together, they dashed down the steps. They didn't stop running until they were safe outside.

At the edge of the iron fence, Dillon spotted the newspaper boy still sitting on his bike, staring.

"Hey, kid!" the boy shouted. "Are you really going to live in *there?*"

"Yeah!" said Dillon loudly, marching down the gravel drive with Sarina. He and Sarina had already agreed to say nothing.

* ❂✳ ❭ *

"Name's Kipper Reeves," the boy said, extending his hand. "Don't you know the story? I'm surprised nosey Wimple didn't tell you."

"What story?" Dillon asked with a smile, shaking his hand. "Oh, this is my sister, Sarina."

Kipper glanced at Sarina, nodded, and then turned to Dillon and said, "Old man Fickle used to own that house, 'til he vanished a year ago. Folks said he was nuts." Kipper stared toward the spooky house with a glazed-over look on his face. "One night, Wimple saw lights glimmering in an upper window. Now she swears it's haunted."

"*Haunted?*" Sarina gaped at Kipper, then shot a nervous glance at her brother.

"It's only a rumor," Kipper assured them. "Some say Fickle had a laboratory hidden in his house. Wimple saw him buy old bottles from Bessie's Antique Shop, and Dr. Hearty saw him carrying copper wire and tubing from Jake's Hardware Store. If you ask me, that weirdo was probably boiling a deadly formula to kill us all—"

"No way!" said Dillon, a light blazing in his eyes, "A *laboratory?* Do you think it's still here?"

Dillon fantasized about Fickle's laboratory. What did it look like? He'd never seen a real one before, except in science class. He remembered only too well dissecting frogs and staring at their dead bodies floating in glass jars.

Meanwhile, Sarina stood quietly. She most likely wouldn't be sleeping by herself that night—or any night—in that creepy house.

"Can't say," Kipper said with a shrug. "One windy day, Fickle disappeared like that." He snapped his fingers. "Nobody knows what became of him. After a year passed by, Smitty closed the case. 'Wasted time and paperwork looking for that old fart!' he'd complain."

"Do you think Fickle was *killed?*" asked Dillon suspiciously, wondering how someone could vanish from a small town.

Kipper shrugged. "Don't know . . . but it doesn't matter now, does it? Folks here would like to, you know, forget it happened." Kipper stared at the two of them, paused, and then looked behind his back.

Dillon tried forcing an image. A distorted jumble flashed before his mind's eye. Slowly, a scene came into focus. There was a man in a silver cloak . . . his one hand wrapped around Fickle's package . . . the other . . . holding a sharpened sword! Sarina's warm voice melted the image, jolting Dillon to conscious awareness.

"What was Mr. Fickle doing before he disappeared?" asked Sarina. This was the first time Sarina had spoken in front of a stranger, but this mystery must have aroused her curiosity.

Kipper dropped his voice to an urgent whisper. "Everyday, Fickle sat in his rocking chair, waiting for his mail to arrive. He stared with these yellowish, beady eyes . . ." Kipper's eyes looked to be a million miles away.

Dillon gulped. He wanted to tell Kipper what had happened earlier, but wasn't sure himself. None of Dillon's previous friends saw spirits. It made life very difficult. He was shunned by classmates and scoffed at by teachers for predicting future test results. Dillon's parents didn't understand his strange abilities—nobody else in the family had them. Dillon wondered. Were his natural-born abilities a gift or a curse? He stood, thinking . . . no, he wasn't about to lose another friend.

A breeze rustled the leaves overhead. Dillon and Sarina listened intently to Kipper's tale. Kipper continued to reenact the whole event according to Ralph Picit's story.

"One day, Picit was making a delivery to old man Fickle's house. Come to think of it, every week Fickle would receive all sorts of strange books and oddly shaped packages in the mail."

"Really?" said Dillon, his eyes bulging. "Like what?" He spent hours reading anything that caught his attention.

"Mostly books on math, science, and astronomy. You know, stupid and boring books. Anyway, it goes like this," he whispered, leaning in closer. "Picit was delivering a large package and ripped around *that* corner." He nudged his head toward the bottom of the hill where Windy Drive intersected with Main Street.

Dillon's heart pounded. He remembered the spirit sifting through a large package. Could it have been Fickle's ghost? Unresolved questions pecked like pigeons at Dillon's head. What was so special about that particular package? Why would someone want to steal it? Why was Fickle possibly murdered because of it? And if he was, where was his body buried?

"The package tumbled, and books slid all over the back of the truck. Picit had to stop and re-tape the box. That's when he saw these, well, peculiar titles."

"Books?" Dillon muttered. "Who would steal or kill for a box of books?"

A short pause followed as Kipper fidgeted on his bike seat, and then he said, "Old man Fickle used to get scientific and technical books, but this time—"

An unexpected wind began kicking up dirt from the street. Although they covered their eyes from the burst of dust, Kipper blabbered on like he couldn't wait to tell someone the news.

"Weird books like *The Lost City of Atlantis, Egyptian Hieroglyphics,* and something about time travel. There were more, but I can't remember them all," choked Kipper, beginning to be distracted by the storm.

The wind became stronger and stronger. Small tree branches fell to the ground, and the telephone wires began to swing uncontrollably. Kipper had to raise his voice over the increasing howl; unseen by them, a black raven swayed over their heads on an unprotected tree branch, as if refusing to fly for cover.

Earlier that day on their car radio, the Allbrights had heard the local station announce clear weather all day. How wrong they were.

A street lamp flickered on, and Windy Drive glowed like a runway. A distant voice came suddenly from the house. An adult, firm sort of voice.

"Dillon!" Mrs. Allbright shouted, straining her voice. "Sarina!"

A narrow tree branch came whipping through the air, missing Kipper's head by an inch. "I better get on," he said at once, reaching forward to shake Dillon's hand. "Great meeting you. Guess we're best friends now." He quickly turned his bike around. "Say, how'd you two like to meet my friends tomorrow?" he asked hoarsely over his shoulder.

"Sure!" squeaked Dillon, thinking it was the best day ever. He felt thrilled, but not at all surprised, to finally have a best friend. He'd have someone to share his ideas. Maybe Kipper could help finish that hover-cart with the vacuum engine. According to the mail-order instructions, it was supposed to levitate six inches off the ground . . .

A strong gust almost knocked him over. He realized it was dangerous to stand there. A runaway trash can was rolling angrily toward him.

When he squinted through his dirt-covered glasses, it appeared calm at the bottom of the hill, as though the storm *only* existed at the top of Windy Drive. What was he thinking? He quickly gave his head a shake and brought his attention to Kipper, who was yelling, "Meet me at Jake's Hardware Store at ten!"

Dillon and Sarina couldn't run fast enough. Their clothes were soaked from the sudden downpour, which felt like ice pellets beating across their backs. In their hurry, they almost collided with the moving van. As they leapt to the side, they couldn't help noticing that the men looked happy to leave.

Meanwhile, from the whipping tree branch, the raven finally flew to dryer ground.

They entered the foyer, shivering. Mrs. Allbright was on her knees wiping up muddy footprints. She sighed when she noticed more mud on the stone floor. "You each get into a hot bath before you get sick," she ordered. "And take off those sneakers."

"But, Mom," whined Dillon in a quivering voice.

Mrs. Allbright's eyes narrowed—there was no mistaking what *that* look meant.

Moments later, in her very own bathroom, Sarina managed to bribe her mother into keeping her company. Even though the story was just a rumor, she wasn't taking any chances.

Dillon filled the antique tub in his private bathroom. He sank into the steaming-hot bath with his favorite container of King Bubbles, which was guaranteed to produce the largest bubbles on the market. He'd hidden the bottle because his mother had said he was too old for bubble baths. But Dillon Allbright didn't care if he was ten years old. He thought bubble baths were fun. Besides, he hadn't seen any age limit written on the container.

He amused himself by attaching a bubble beard and a pirate's hat. He was One-eyed Willie, captain of a large fleet of pirate ships. He was preparing to capture a group of shipping vessels filled with gold and fine jewels . . .

After his fantasy victory, he closed his eyes and thought about Fickle's laboratory and the unresolved mystery behind his disappearance. The warm water soothed his body, which led his mind into his imagination. He turned it all over in his head, submerged among the shrinking bubbles, until his fingers looked like dried prunes.

A tree branch attacked the window, thrashing its fury against the pane. Suddenly, Dillon felt wide-awake. In his frightened state, every shadow moved like a ghost. Was it Fickle's spirit or just his imagination playing tricks on him?

He sat up quickly and reached for his fogged-up glasses. His heart raced as he craned his head around the misty room. He saw a shimmering presence, but when he blinked, it was gone. Even though he was used to seeing transparent bodies, it still startled him. An icy draft swirled around the tub. He rubbed his arms, shivering in the cold water.

Moments later, he saw something at the opposite end of the tub. "What the—?"

Dillon sat frozen with fear as the color drained from his face. He stared intently at what looked like a sword made of soap bubbles. He watched it slowly emerge from the surface of the water to eye level. Remarkably, it remained intact, as though an invisible arm under the foamy water held it steady.

Soon after, the sword abruptly collapsed with a splattering splash. The scene looked like a ship sunk tragically below the icy waters, leaving only the remnant of a swirling funnel.

Dillon was amazed. He'd never seen anything like it. Was he imagining all of it? He was beginning to doubt himself. Maybe he was going mad. Could he have soaked in the tub so long it affected his mind? And if the sword was really there, did it have anything to do with his strange vision—or the duel he'd heard earlier?

His eyes remained fixed on the spot where the sword had been. His mind was spinning. Should he chance it and stand up?

I want to get out of here, he thought. *If I take a deep breath, I'll be okay. I'll just count to three. One—what if my legs don't move?—Two—just do it—Three!*

Dillon sprang from the tub, yanked the drain plug, and grabbed a towel on his way out, leaving behind a trail of watery footprints. He decided not to mention anything to anyone. He didn't want people thinking he was seeing things. After all, who would believe him? Nobody ever did.

The rain mysteriously vanished as nightfall crept over the hill. A cool breeze swayed two lanterns that hung off the pillars. Silence filled the air, broken only by droplets of water trickling down the leaves.

It was midnight and the Allbrights were asleep. Sarina was nestled safely in between her parents, while a few doors down, Dillon lay awake, rethinking the eerie incident. Was Fickle's ghost attempting to scare him? Was Fickle a distraught spirit that wanted his life and house back?

Dillon tried putting it out of his head, but his analytical mind challenged him to dig deeper. And the consequences always led him into a pile of dog dung, a messy state where he'd ask more and more questions—which was the wrong thing to do in Willow Creek.

Even when Dillon drifted off into an uneasy sleep, the unexplained occurrences repeated themselves within his dreams. His last, comforting thought before he fell asleep was that even if it *had* been Fickle's ghost, his mother always said, "The dead can't hurt you. It's the living you should be leery of."

Willow Creek was the last place you'd expect anything unusual or mysterious to happen. But at this very moment, unseen by anyone, a figure stood in silence among the shadows of the iron gates.

CHAPTER THREE

NORTON'S PASS

An annoying bird woke Dillon from his restless sleep. He glanced over to his nightstand. There was a pause, and then he realized what he was seeing.

"It can't be nine-thirty already!"

They'd only half an hour to get to Jake's Hardware Store. Dillon's alarm clock wasn't working, again. He thought he fixed it, but why did he have one piece remaining?

He quickly got dressed and, with one sneaker untied, scampered into Sarina's room, which was across the hall. He'd heard his father place her there earlier that morning.

His sister was snuggled into a fetal position deep within the soft blankets. "Sarina!" he whispered loudly, shaking her awake. He tugged at her blankets, while trying to tie his sneaker. "Hurry or we'll be late!"

"Where am I?" she yawned, looking disoriented. "What time is it? Wasn't your alarm clock working?"

Dillon shook his head. His sister despised being late to anything.

"C'mon," he said impatiently, trying to find her clothes. He tossed her a pair of socks that were stuffed neatly in her sneakers. "I'll get the bikes out of the garage and leave a note for Mom. Meet me outside, okay?"

Sarina tiredly nodded.

They raced down Windy Drive, pedaling as fast as their short legs would move. They rounded the corner onto Main Street and passed Bessie's Antique Shop, Betty Lou's Kitchen, Al's Grocery Market, and the public library.

Dillon's eyes widened when he saw a sign that read Charlie's Candy Store. Fancy glass jars, overflowing with sweets, were displayed in the window. Kids were loitering outside the door, waiting for the store to open.

From a distance, they saw Kipper talking with a boy and girl. The thin, dark-haired boy looked about ten, the same age as Dillon and Kipper. The short, curly-headed girl was chunky and seemed to be Sarina's age.

"Right on time, Allbright," said Kipper smugly, glancing at his watch. "I like a person's who's punctual. It shows good character." Kipper nodded to his friends.

Dillon lowered his head, trying to hide his smile, while his sister shot him a look. When he felt her cold stare melt away, he looked up. A sign overhead said Jake's Hardware Store.

"This here is Tommy Flick and his sister, Tara," said Kipper, pointing to the Flicks. "They live on Oak Tree Road. There's old tires, broken lawn mowers, and other junk scattered over their lawn." Kipper laughed. "You'd swear it was designated the town's junkyard."

Dillon's smile broadened, but not because of Kipper's words. The two kids he'd predicted he'd meet, whose last name started with the letter *F*, were standing before him.

"How's it going?" said Tommy, reaching out his hand toward Dillon. Obviously, he was ignoring Kipper's crude comments. "Heard you moved into old man Fickle's house. Did you hear the story?" His eyes widened.

"Yeah," muttered Dillon, shaking his hand. "Kipper told us yesterday. Oh, this is my sister, Sarina."

Tommy turned toward Sarina and stared. He looked disappointed to see another girl. Tara, on the other hand, appeared happy to meet a new friend, especially a *girl* friend. She stuck out her tongue at her older brother, but he didn't seem to notice.

"Um, hello," Sarina said in a low tone, her face turning a shade of pink.

After a few moments of silence, Kipper made a suggestion.

"I got an idea. Let's ride to the creek." He kicked off on his bike. "C'mon, Dillon. I'll show you our secret place!"

The creek was just outside of town, below Norton's Pass, a dirt road that merged into a single trail through the woods. Just before the creek, in a rundown shack, lived Lady Norton. Folks called her a witch. Harriet Wimple had told everyone she talked to animals. She'd seen the old witch conversing with a raven sitting on a lamppost in front of Al's Grocery Market.

A short time ago, Lady Norton had concocted a smoking, stinky-smelling formula and had given it to Dr. Hearty. Dr. Hearty wondered uncomfortably how she knew about his sick patient. He wouldn't accept her concoction and escorted her out. "What's this world coming to!" He'd lift his droopy pants up over his fat stomach. "Magic formulas? It's all hocus-pocus if you ask me!"

They hadn't seen much of Lady Norton since, but occasionally she'd wander into town to buy supplies, dragging her carved walking stick.

Kipper called over his shoulder, "Just up ahead!"

The wide dirt path narrowed suddenly at the edge of the woods.

"Welcome, newcomers, to Norton's Pass!" Kipper announced. "I'll go first and—oh, by the way—do try to keep up. I'm not responsible if Lady Norton grabs you and keeps you captive forever." He grinned wickedly. "You never know what can happen. Isn't that right, Tommy?"

Tommy nodded. "One day, I heard this ghostly wailing—this piercing cry," he said dramatically, staring blankly into the woods. "Smitty thinks Fickle's buried here, but said it's too much trouble to hunt for his remains."

Dillon knew the story was false, but had an inkling Tara would imagine a gruesome scenario. Fickle's half-dead body crawling along the narrow path, snatching Tara's leg as she pedaled by . . . dragging her off . . . sucking on her blood to keep himself alive . . .

Tara gave herself a shake, gulped, and said, "I . . . I think I'll go back. I just remembered that—"

"You're just scared," snapped Tommy. "Go ahead. Go home and play with the sissies instead." Tommy cradled an imaginary doll and pretended to kiss its face.

"I'm not a sissy," she stammered, her voice faltering. "W-Why do I always have to be last?" She folded her arms in protest. "It's not fair!"

"If you'd stop eating all those candy bars, maybe you could keep up," retorted Tommy.

Tara shot Tommy a piercing look.

"You can ride in front of me, Tara," said Dillon thoughtfully, "so you won't be last."

"Don't worry, Tara," Sarina whispered, leaning over. "I'm sure Tommy didn't mean it. You can ride in between Dillon and me, if you'd like."

"Let's go!" barked Kipper, starting to pedal. "We don't have all day!"

Tara seemed confused by their warm hospitality. She must not have been treated well. After all, she lived with her pain-in-the-butt brother.

Kipper and Tommy were gone. The other three had to pedal fast to catch up. Just like they'd promised, Sarina took the lead, Tara rode in the middle, and Dillon tailed closely behind.

The air became damp as they went deeper into the foliage. Sunlight filtered brightly through the openings in the trees, revealing the vast spread of land. They hurried along the uneven trail, not daring to stop. Dillon heard Tara talking to herself.

"I'm *fine* . . . everything's *fine* . . . it's a lovely day . . ."

Just up ahead, the two boys were huddled together, discussing something.

"What's going on?" Dillon asked curiously, skidding his bike alongside them.

"Lady Norton's old shack," whispered Kipper, pointing to a clearing. "Everyone keep your trap shut or she'll hear us. She probably already knows we're here." He looked cautiously around.

The shack was set back about fifty feet from the trail. Dingy windows stood to each side of the door, and an uneven pile of cut wood sat on the porch. Moss grew in the gutters, and torn branches and soggy leaves blanketed the entire roof.

Dillon wondered. How could someone live in such a primitive-looking place? It looked like it was built with random pieces of scrap wood. An aroma of wood smoke roamed up his nostrils.

A roaring fire burned by the porch, and dangling over the center was an iron kettle. Dillon watched the boiling water release blue smoke and cough tiny green bubbles.

Then nearly everyone fell off their seats when Tommy shouted. "What was that!"

Tara's heart thumped wildly. "What's the matter?" she said at once. "Tell me!"

"Boooo! Lady Norton's coming to get you, Tara!" Tommy waved his hands in the air.

Tara's face burned as she lunged at her older brother. But— CRASH! She landed hard on the ground with a solid thud. Tommy happily slipped away, pedaling down the trail.

"Are you okay?" Sarina asked Tara in a concerned voice.

But Tara didn't answer. She remounted her bike, looking like she was devising a payback plan. They pedaled on, not knowing that someone had been watching them from behind a thick berry bush.

A half mile down, past a row of pine trees, they came to a sunny clearing. Tommy was sitting on a rocky ledge that extended over a raging waterfall. Since they'd discovered it, it was *their* secret place— no parents, teachers, or pesty little brats allowed.

"Here it is!" cried Kipper proudly, looking over at Dillon. "What do you think?"

"It . . . it's cool," said Dillon breathlessly. "Real cool."

They spent most of the day exchanging stories, telling jokes, and soaking up the sun. Kipper mentioned for the tenth time the mystery surrounding Henry Fickle's disappearance. Each time, Kipper stretched the truth further and further, like stretching a rubber band.

"What do you suppose happened to Mr. Fickle?" Sarina asked, watching a parade of leaves wrestle down a narrow waterway. "How can someone vanish without leaving evidence behind?"

"Hard to say," said Tommy with a shrug. "That's the mystery. I think—" Tommy stopped as though he heard something, but this time everyone ignored him.

At that moment, Dillon felt anxious to reveal his vision, but Kipper started talking.

"Did you find anything in that rickety house?" Kipper asked Dillon.

Dillon's heart sank. It had been the perfect opportunity, but now it was gone. Instead he said, "No, but I think I know where the laboratory might be."

There was dead silence as everyone quickly turned toward Dillon.

"Dad's office. You know, behind one of the bookcases." His mouth crinkled into a smile.

Everyone's eyes gleamed. It appeared Dillon had brightened up a rather hopeless situation. Without taking her eyes off him, Tara felt in her bike sack and took out a bulging sandwich. She listened intently, as the mayonnaise smeared her cheeks.

"Wh-o-a," said Kipper, straightening up. "A secret button is usually under a desk. I'd bet my new pair of designer underwear it'll turn the bookcase around." Kipper smiled brightly.

Tara gagged suddenly on her half-eaten sandwich, Tommy turned a shade of green, and Dillon coughed at the thought of winning Kipper's used underwear.

"So-o-o," echoed a deep, screechy voice. "You're searching for the laboratory, eh!"

They jumped about a foot in the air. Sarina screamed, and Tara's to-die-for sandwich slipped from her hand. The floating voice sounded like Lady Norton—or was it Henry Fickle? It was hard to tell. For the first time, Kipper looked shaken.

"What did you say, Dillon?" he whispered, grabbing his arm. "You said something—didn't you?" His knees started buckling.

"It wasn't me," muttered Dillon, looking wildly around.

Since there was no escape, they accepted their fate with gritted teeth. Huddled closely together, they stepped down from the ledge and searched through the glare of the late afternoon sun.

The woods suddenly went quiet, as if time stood still.

One frightening thought penetrated Dillon's mind. He was about to confront the witch or the ghost—both he'd been told to fear the most. Somehow, he managed to find his lost voice. "Who . . . who's there . . . show yourself!"

They all screamed when a large raven screeched overhead. Before Dillon had time to think, a whirlwind lifted the leaves and swirled them in the air. The miniature funnel traveled over to the pine trees . . .

Walking through it, as if in slow motion, was Lady Norton.

SIR DUKE

"It's *her!*" cried Kipper. "Run for your life!"

But it was too late. Their eyes met Lady Norton's. They tried desperately to move, but couldn't get their legs to follow. They were frozen like statues, petrified with fear. Nobody talked except Tara, who was babbling frantically about how they'd be boiled alive and strained into a formula bottle. Any second, she'd turn them into something horrible.

"H-How long were you there listening?" stuttered Tommy, standing behind Kipper.

"Long enough to hear you talking about good old Henry," thundered Lady Norton, waving her walking stick at them. "Henry happens to be a dear and, well, old friend of mine."

Lady Norton was short, plump, and old. Her black hair was streaked with white like a skunk's. She wore a shabby green dress that was tied with a purple sash. And around her thick neck dangled all sorts of stones and crystals. She looked very strict.

Dillon's first impression was this wasn't someone to make mad. He swallowed hard. "Miss Norton . . . I mean . . . Lady Norton," he muttered. "We were wondering about Mr. Fickle . . . you know . . . interested in finding his laboratory. It might explain how he vanished."

Lady Norton laughed out loud. Her voice reverberated through the woods, breaking the tension in the air. Everyone looked some-what relieved, but unsure of what to expect.

"Why yes, Dillon," she said, still chuckling as she flopped herself down on a nearby rock. "What would *you* like to know about Henry's laboratory?"

"H-How did you know my name? I don't believe we've met."

Lady Norton's face formed into a smile, which looked quite pleas-ant. She placed her walking stick on the ground, as if to call a truce. With an eyebrow half raised and a gleam in her eye, she gently brushed her streaked hair from her face.

"Well, Mr. Allbright, I've known all your names since you were born—and the exact times and birthdays." Her eyes lingered on each of them.

Kipper looked surprised by her bold words.

"That's impossible! The Allbrights just moved here yesterday, and you weren't even there!"

Dillon was shocked. Could Lady Norton be like *him?* After all, only someone with good intuition could predict such things.

Luckily for all their sakes, Lady Norton remained smiling. "I wasn't there personally, Mr. Reeves, but my Duke was."

"Since you seem to know our birthdays and times," drilled Tommy, giving a sideways look at Kipper, his expression changing from puzzlement to amusement, "then what's mine?"

"Certainly, Mr. Flick," she said confidently, scanning his body. Her eyes disappeared behind her eyelids. "You were born on November 22 at 6:19 p.m.—Dr. Hearty delivered you, and you have a birthmark on the left side of your bottom." Her eyes rolled back into place. "Is that about right, Mr. Flick?"

Tommy's smirk was wiped clean. By the look on his pasty white face, she was telling the truth. The private information Lady Norton had mentioned was printed on Tommy's birth certificate. As for the birthmark, his friends didn't know about it, because he'd been too embarrassed to tell them.

The girls giggled, while Kipper's eyes popped out.

"What's so funny?" Tommy asked furiously, glaring at the girls. "Shut up!"

One by one, Lady Norton told them their birthdays and time they were born. How she knew about such personal things was incomprehensible to their limited minds, except Dillon's. To Dillon, this was a common, everyday occurrence. He stood, thinking. He desperately wanted to speak to Lady Norton in private. Maybe she could answer a few of his questions.

"Who's Duke?" asked Sarina politely, edging closer.

"Ah yes, Miss Sarina, come sit by me. Don't be afraid now, little miss, I won't hurt you."

Everyone looked shocked to see that shy little Sarina wasn't scared. After all, Lady Norton was a witch. The others hesitated, but eventually shuffled in closer to listen.

"Sir Duke is my raven companion," she said, smiling proudly. "We get together and chat. Didn't you see him in your oak tree when you were talking to Mr. Reeves yesterday?"

Sarina shook her head, and then quickly glanced at Dillon. Tommy kept rolling his eyes, as though he thought Lady Norton needed therapy.

"I got word city folks moved into Henry's house. Sir Duke informed me you'd been wondering about his laboratory and discussing what had become of him." Lady Norton abruptly turned toward Tommy. "Oh, by the way, Mr. Flick, I don't need a shrink, but thank you for your concern."

Tommy's white face turned deep red. Their heads turned toward Tommy, but no one spoke.

"You have a talking bird?" said Tara, holding her hands to her hips. "Birds don't talk!"

"Heavens no, child," laughed Lady Norton. "I speak to Sir Duke telepathically—"

"You mean with your mind?" Dillon butted in, pushing his glasses up on his nose. "I know about that . . . I mean . . . I read about that in the library."

"That's witch stuff!" gasped Tommy abruptly, pointing his finger at Lady Norton. "Pop says it ain't normal . . . and you're a . . . a *witch!*"

Everyone swallowed hard. Kipper looked like he wanted to elbow his foolish friend, but seemed frozen. Any moment, Lady Norton would turn them into frogs . . .

But instead, her eyebrows arched. "Interesting, isn't it?" She stared long at Tommy. "What makes me a witch? Do you see me holding a broomstick?"

Tommy glanced at her walking stick, paused, and then seemed to change his mind. "Umm, well," he muttered, shuffling his feet over the same spot. "It's the way you dress. And those stones around your neck. Pop says nobody else wears them. And those stinky potions— and you talk to your bird in your head."

"I see," she said in a faint tone, staring blankly into space, and then turned. "Is that it?"

Tommy lowered his head. "I guess," he mumbled, after a few seconds of quiet thought.

"That's what Mom says," added Kipper, looking over at Tommy. "The townsfolk, too."

"Let me see . . ." Lady Norton said slowly. "How do you suppose dressing differently would make me a witch? Why should I dress like everyone else?" Her eyes lingered on Tommy, but he abruptly looked away.

After an uncomfortable silence, Kipper spoke.

"I reckon you're right—but what about those stones?"

"What's so bad about wearing them?" she asked, rubbing her quartz crystal. "They're a part of nature. They radiate a wonderful vibration, don't you think?"

Dillon didn't have a clue what she meant about *vibration,* but it didn't seem to matter. He was beginning to feel more comfortable with her. At least she hadn't turned him into a slimy frog.

"About my smelly potions. First of all, they're called healing remedies," she said diligently, pointing around with her stick. "Compliments of nature herself. I gather different flowers, herbs, and barks, according to a person's ailment. I don't add eye of newt, claw of bird, and especially, no dragon's liver." Lady Norton cringed.

"Are you serious, Miss Norton?" asked Tara in disbelief. "No crawly things?"

"No, child, no of course not," she chuckled.

"You don't use poisonous stuff?" said Tommy. "But, Dr. Hearty said—"

Before Tommy could say another word, Lady Norton blew her top. The air suddenly was filled with tension. "Rufeous is a medical doctor!"

she thundered. "He's trained to follow the practice of the medical board! He's set in his ways and thinks with his limited mind! Anything outside of this must be unnatural or useless!" She cracked her stick against the base of the ledge and flashed her eyes furiously toward town. "Stupid man!"

Tommy scuttled miserably behind the others. Tara gave him the evil eye, then suddenly elbowed him in the ribs. Tommy had gotten the message.

"How did the Indians heal themselves?" she raged on. "There weren't any drugstores in those days!"

"I get it," chimed in Dillon. "Dr. Hearty told everyone you're a witch because you don't follow *his* rules. Isn't that right, Miss Norton?"

Lady Norton forced her face into a smile, as if she were still struggling with her anger. "Yes, Dillon!" She leaped up and waved her stick in the air like a music conductor, while her feet tapped along to a beat. "I believe you're right!"

The air was calm and relaxed once again. Tommy seemed ready to speak but was silenced by a nudge from Kipper.

"You can't believe everything you hear," said Kipper, moving his eyes from Tommy to Lady Norton. "But Wimple was right about seeing you talking with Sir Duke."

Lady Norton nodded and said, "You're quite right, Mr. Reeves."

"I don't understand, Miss Norton," said Sarina in an unsettled voice. "What about the smoky and stinky potion?"

"Well," said Lady Norton. "Sir Duke informed me a young girl had been ill. I made a batch of my secret remedy, but Rufeous shoved me out of his office. If I made the little one better . . . no, Rufeous wouldn't hear of it." A disappointed look crept over Lady Norton's face. She shook her head and then continued.

"The combination of ingredients in that particular remedy causes it to smell like rotten eggs. And the smoke was caused by a powerful *thought form* I added for an extra boost." She managed a smile, then suddenly looked serious. "Mind you, it's all very effective."

"A *what?*" everyone said together.

She leaned in closer as if the town could hear. "I think thoughts of wellness and add them to my remedy. An extra boost of healthy thoughts can induce healing, you see." Lady Norton looked like she was thinking. "Of course, the person has to want to get better . . ."

Kipper, Tommy, and Tara looked puzzled. Sarina kept smiling and nodding her head. She probably had no clue what Lady Norton was saying but wanted to look polite. Dillon didn't understand the part about adding *thought forms* as an ingredient but concluded anything was possible.

Dillon pondered over a few questions. What would happen if he thought of *death,* and then splashed it in the mixture? Could he kill the person? How did she actually place her thoughts in the kettle? And what was the procedure for adding *thought forms* to a remedy if you couldn't see them? This old woman was definitely not like any psychic he'd read about. He just had to talk to her.

Sarina's eyes suddenly welled with tears. "That's awful," she sniffed. "Dr. Hearty lied to everyone." Sarina took a tissue from her pocket and dabbed her eyes.

"Now, now young miss," Lady Norton said, patting her gently on the back. "Who will the townsfolk believe? Rufeous Hearty, a beloved doctor, or an old lady who lives in the woods?"

"Don't you want to clear your name and set everyone straight?" urged Kipper, getting to his feet. "We could help." He looked anxiously at the others, who nodded.

Lady Norton collapsed on the rocky ledge and sighed very deeply. She quickly wiped a small tear from the corner of her eye.

"For a civilization to survive, it *must* learn to accept people and their differences, otherwise there will always be conflict. Did you know fighting with others takes place because of differences? Wars and battles are fought because someone is defending their opinion? How much more time will be wasted before we learn to get along?"

Sarina and Kipper nodded.

From that moment, Lady Norton became their friend. She was allowed to sit on *their* ledge. A flutter of wings caught their attention as Sir Duke landed next to Lady Norton.

"Ah, there you are, Sir Duke. Nice of you to join us." The two stared deeply at each other for several minutes, until Lady Norton burst out laughing and Sir Duke squawked loudly.

"Sir Duke told me Harriet Wimple has gotten her hair colored at

Florence's Beauty Parlor. But instead of light brown, her hair turned carrot orange! Apparently, Florence apologized for using the wrong dye, but Harriet went storming out of her shop, telling anyone who'd listen."

Everyone smiled widely. It wasn't too often Harriet got what she deserved.

"About my talking to Sir Duke with my mind. Mental telepathy has been known since ancient times. We use it every day, but some aren't aware they're doing it, you see."

"We do?" asked Tara. "How?"

"Well, have you ever thought about someone and next thing you know, they're calling you on the telephone?" she asked them. "Your thoughts are projected like radio waves, and sometimes the other person tunes in."

"Awesome!" said Tommy, turning to Kipper. "That happens to me a lot. Just when I'm about to call Kipper, he calls me or vice versa. Mom calls it a coincidence."

Lady Norton listened. Her dark eyes glimmered in the setting sun. Sir Duke stood tall and quiet, basking in the last rays. His beak crinkled in a funny kind of way, as if he were still laughing at Wimple's carrot top. They all forgot the time, as dark shadows stretched across the creek.

"Run along now, children," urged Lady Norton, standing to stretch her back. "It's quite late, but I'm sure we'll meet again." There was a bright light in her eyes.

"Oh, Miss Norton!" breathed Sarina, gazing at the orange and purple hues reflected off her crystal. "Couldn't we stay a little longer?"

Lady Norton's silence and gentle smile told them there was always another day.

Dillon's heart sank. He hadn't had a chance to speak with Lady Norton. He'd have to wait for another opportunity. When he swung himself onto his bike, a sudden thought struck him. He quickly turned and said, "You forgot to tell us what happened to Henry and his labora—"

But Lady Norton was gone. Instead, Dillon was staring at an unoccupied space. She departed so suddenly and silently you'd think she sank below the ground.

When they passed by the shack, they saw through the thin curtains an outline of a bird sitting on someone's shoulder. Dillon was sure Tommy thought Lady Norton had flown home on her walking stick.

They were almost out of the woods when they heard a loud shriek: "HENRY'S LABORATORY . . . WAIT FOR THE FULL MOON!"

The shrieky voice reverberated through the air, soaring above the treetops. They sat at the edge of the dirt path, trying to figure out what the words meant.

"That was Lady Norton!" announced Kipper, turning his head toward the others. "What was she telling us about old man Fickle's laboratory?"

"She said to wait for the full moon," said Dillon, staring into the darkened woods.

"What does that mean?" Tara asked Dillon, as if the moon held possibilities.

"I'm not sure, but it must have something to do with Henry's laboratory."

"How can the *moon* have anything to do with it?" grunted Tommy, shifting on his seat. "I don't get it."

Thoughts were zinging in the air until a faint voice interrupted them.

"Miss Norton wouldn't have mentioned the laboratory if it weren't *there*," said Sarina in a soft tone, pointing her small index finger. Her face was bright with anticipation.

Everyone stared at Sarina, while Dillon followed the direction of her finger, which was pointing to town. It wasn't long before he was struck by a sudden idea.

"Of course! Don't you see? The laboratory *is* somewhere in our house, although I can't figure out the part about the full moon!"

Dillon pondered Lady Norton's words. He tried to think of a simple solution, but nothing came to mind. His brain hurt from thinking so much. Finally he gave in and made a suggestion. "There's only one way to find out. Let's meet at our house after dinner . . ."

Their faces glowed with enthusiasm, and their longing eyes revealed it was a wonderful idea. With not another word, they briskly pedaled to town, waving as they went their separate ways.

Meanwhile, sitting noiselessly on a towering tree branch, the meddlesome Sir Duke had been eavesdropping on their entire conversation.

CHAPTER FIVE

THE MYSTERIOUS NOTE

During dinner, Dillon and Sarina stuffed down their food, periodically glancing at the clock. Finally, Dillon conjured up the nerve to ask his mother if he could invite his friends over.

"I don't see why not. Come to think of it, where were you both today?" she inquired.

Ding-dong!

Dillon and Sarina didn't answer—they were racing to the front door.

Mrs. Allbright sat there shaking her head. "What do you think of that, Norman?"

"What?" he muttered, engrossed in his newspaper. "What's the matter, Trudy?"

"Nothing, Norman, just nothing!" she snapped, getting up to do the dishes. "Go back to your paper, Norman." Every now and then she threw him dirty looks and mumbled words like "should have listened to my sister . . . had to move us to the middle of nowhere," and "might as well talk to the wall . . ."

Dillon yanked open the arched door. He was beaming at his friends. Nothing could have pleased him more than to see them all there.

"Aren't you going to let us in, Dillon?" said Kipper, trying to peer inside.

"Oh, yes, come in," he said, while glancing over at the kitchen. "Mom said it was okay." He gave a thumbs up.

All three of them stepped cautiously into the candlelit foyer. Their eyes roamed up the wooden staircase and stopped at the hanging chandelier. They'd always wanted to know what it was like inside. They stood in silence for a brief moment, hypnotized by the flaming candles' dance up the walls. At any moment, Fickle's ghost would swoop down the staircase . . .

Tara flinched when an armored head glared at her. Where was the entrance to the laboratory? Could Fickle's ghost be guarding it? A loud clattering of dishes brought them back to conscious awareness.

"Where's your father's office?" Kipper asked Dillon in a low voice.

"It's this way," said Sarina at once, walking through the living room.

"Better hurry before they finish up," Dillon whispered, glancing over Tommy's head. "Dad reads the newspaper, while Mom sits with her cup of tea and fashion magazines." Dillon rolled his eyes toward the ceiling.

Tall, narrow doors concealed Dr. Allbright's office. Dillon carefully clicked them open and switched on the lights. They secretly slipped inside like thieves in the night, quietly closing the doors behind.

The large room had an eleven-foot ceiling trimmed with antique molding. Two matching leather chairs faced a small fireplace. A long mahogany desk was piled with a stack of papers. And a wall of bookcases touched the ceiling—there must have been thousands of books.

"Where do we start?" moaned Tara, clapping her hand to her mouth.

"Everyone spread out," said Kipper, walking toward the desk, "and look for something." He reached his hands underneath, sliding his fingers slowly along the entire length.

Dillon searched the shelves with Tommy, sliding books back and forth, while the girls looked behind pictures and underneath oriental rugs.

But no secret button or entrance to the laboratory was found. After fifteen minutes of fruitless searching, Dillon heard heavy footsteps clunking across the stone foyer.

"It's Dad!"

There was no place to hide except under the desk, but they couldn't all fit there. The footsteps were getting louder—

"Quick," whispered Dillon, scurrying toward a row of windows. "Get behind these curtains."

They flattened themselves behind ugly-looking orange drapes and fell silent. Dillon's heart pounded, while Sarina held her breath. Behind the next curtain, Tommy held his hand over Tara's mouth to stop her from screaming, and Kipper was still as a statue. A sudden thought struck Dillon—he'd left the lights on.

The door was flung wide open and Dr. Allbright shuffled in.

"What the—?"

Dr. Allbright walked quickly over to his desk. "Waste of good electricity," he said aloud, sounding displeased with himself.

Through a split in the drapes, Dillon saw his father staring at a piece of paper, while mumbling more words. He strained to hear what he was saying, but his father was out of earshot. By his tone of voice, Dillon figured it was a hefty bill.

Dr. Allbright started to exit the room and then suddenly spun around. His eyes darted toward the drapes.

A bead of sweat formed on Dillon's forehead.

Dr. Allbright paused, as though he saw something. He shook his head, turned, switched off the lights, and closed the door.

Dillon listened to his footsteps dying away. That had been close, too close.

"Is he gone?" Tara asked, breathing deeply. She peeked into the pitch-black room, gasping.

"Shhh!" hissed Tommy. "They might hear you!"

They clung tight to each other and felt their way to the door.

"Let's face it, there's nothing here or we would have found it by now," said Kipper halfheartedly, eyeing the sliver of light from the door. "The laboratory has to be somewhere else."

"Kipper's right," said Tommy, wiping sweat from his brow. "We searched this entire room. Besides, what if your Dad comes back?"

Dillon paused for a moment and then said, "I have an idea." He stared at the faint outlines of their bodies and turned toward a petite one. "Let's take them upstairs, Sarina."

Dillon pressed his ear against the doors, listening for sounds.

When he cracked it open, he saw an empty room. In the distance, he heard his father saying something to his mother.

They slipped out the door, moving swiftly and silently. One by one, they crept up the steps. Everything went smoothly, until Dillon stepped on the annoying loose board.

Mrs. Allbright's voice called out. "Who's there? Dillon, is that you?"

Dillon motioned to the others to press on, while he headed toward the kitchen. He fought to keep his face straight as he rounded the corner.

"It's me, Mom," he said, wiping sweat from his face. "I wanted something to . . . to drink."

"What are you up to now, Dillon?" Mrs. Allbright asked irritably, looking up from her magazine.

"We're busy, Mom." He hastily filled a glass with lemonade. "You know . . . showing them my stuff." He tried not to look guilty, but his smirk kept on trying to surface.

"Your friends have to leave in an hour." Her head quickly lowered. (She was trying to read an interesting article.)

"Oh, Mom! Can't it be a little longer? Dad—"

Dr. Allbright grunted.

"You have until nine," she said firmly, peering over the pages. "Are you involving those poor kids with another one of your brainy ideas?"

But Dillon didn't answer. He was gulping down his lemonade in one swallow. He set the glass on the counter and said, "Gotta go." His smirk finally surfaced in the hallway.

It wasn't too often Dillon could convince his mother he wasn't involved in anything out of the ordinary. He was always up to something crazy or dangerous. How could Mrs. Allbright forget the time her son built a flying contraption in the garage? Dillon had bribed Sarina into joining him on a large rubber donut tied to helium balloons. "It's my best invention ever," he had told Sarina. Any minute, they'd fly around the neighborhood. But it never happened. And the time Dillon jumped off the garage roof with cardboard wings and ended up with a swollen ankle. No, Mrs. Allbright knew better.

Just before his parents' bedroom, Dillon yanked open a squeaky door. It took forever to persuade Tara up the steep stairs—finding

Fickle's lab didn't seem important to her anymore. "It looks scary up there!" she protested. "I-I'm not going!"

"Shhh!" hissed Tommy, forcing her up the steps. "Up you go!"

Dillon found the light switch, and together they cautiously climbed the narrow steps. Tara couldn't help but notice the cobwebs dangling from the walls.

The room was still, as though it were waiting for them to arrive. On the far side was a round window that faced the front of the house. It seemed no one had been up in the dusty attic for quite some time. It looked untouched since Fickle's disappearance.

"That's just great," groaned Tommy, moving cobwebs aside with his hand. "It's empty."

"I don't understand," said Dillon as a sudden surge of anger reddened his face. "If it wasn't in Dad's office, and it's not here, then where else could it be?" Dillon tried to *see* the laboratory with his psychic abilities, but the harder he tried, the more distorted it got.

Although he felt grim, he wasn't going to give in, not just yet. Nothing was going to dampen his spirits, he vowed. His mind was scanning for a plan of action when Tara's scream disrupted his thinking.

"Euww!" shouted Tara, thrashing about. "Spiders! Get them off me!" She tripped over a protruding nail and barreled across the room into a heart-stopping crash. Luckily, the Allbrights had the volume cranked up on their TV so you could have heard it from town.

Suddenly, Tara looked as though she'd seen Santa Claus.

"What is it?" Dillon asked at once.

"*Look* everyone," she said happily, snatching up a dusty object. "Look what I found." She blew the dust from a picture frame.

The portrait of an elderly man with a scruffy beard and yellowish eyes glared at her. She gasped. The shifty eyes looked crazy and seemed to follow her every move.

"It's old man Fickle," spoke Kipper, snatching the frame from Tara's hands.

"He still looks nuts," said Tommy with a grin. "Check it out."

"If it wasn't for Tara sliding across the floor on her butt . . . well, we wouldn't have found it," said Kipper proudly, giving her a firm whack on the back. "I say three cheers for Tara!"

Everyone cheered together. "Tara rules! Tara rules! Tara rules!"

Tara's cheeks turned a bright shade of pink. This was the perfect opportunity to earn some respect. But it wasn't to be.

"Can I see?" Dillon asked Kipper with an eager expression.

Kipper handed it over as he glanced at his watch. "Holy smokes—it's eight-thirty!" He got to his feet. "C'mon, we better get moving."

But Dillon wasn't listening. He wasn't concerned about the time or the consequences of getting caught. Instead, he was absorbing every detail of Fickle's appearance, running his fingers slowly over the photo. He felt like he'd met Henry before, but couldn't recall where. And he remembered something else. Since he was six, a brilliant sword kept appearing in his dreams. He closed his eyes and saw it again more clearly than ever before. He blinked his eyes open, and when he flipped the frame over, he saw something.

"Look at this!"

A yellowed paper was taped to the back. On it was writing in emerald-green ink. He paused, gazed around the room, cleared his throat, and read:

It's not what it appears. My walls have ears.
If you should find this note at night,
make sure the moon is full delight.

Dillon looked intently at the aged note, trying to decipher its meaning. After a few minutes of silence, he tore his eyes away from it to look excitedly at the others. "Both this note and Lady Norton's message mention a full moon, right?" He blinked anxiously at them.

Tommy straightened up and said, "So, what's your point?"

"Let him talk, Tommy!" said Tara hotly, trying to kick her brother's leg. But he was too fast. "You always interrupt people when they're trying to say something."

"Knock it off!" said Kipper in a harsh tone. "The kid has something important to say." He pushed Dillon in the arm. "Go on, Dillon."

Dillon nodded. "I believe there's a correlation between Lady Norton's words and this note. Don't you see? They both mention a full moon. Something's going to happen, but only when the moon is full."

"You're right," agreed Kipper. "The moon's not full tonight, but according to my almanac, tomorrow it will be."

"What does 'walls have ears' mean?" Tommy asked impatiently. "I don't get it."

"Someone's listening," Tara said in a low voice, looking warily around the room. She looked as though she heard a faint voice from behind the walls saying, "*Tara . . . help me . . . I need to get out . . .*"

Dillon hid the frame behind a wide wooden post, and as he turned away, he could have sworn the image gave a smile. But as soon as he looked back, the smile was gone. Maybe he was imagining it; maybe not.

A chill whisked through the room, reminding him of recent events. A storm that existed *only* on the hill of Windy Drive? Random chills smothering the warm air? A sword made of soap bubbles? An invisible duel? And a smile, a smile across a portrait . . .

A grin broke across Dillon's face. He wondered if Fickle's ghost was pleased they'd found the mysterious note? He walked over to the staircase and wasn't surprised to see everyone bickering. He heard Tara saying, "I scraped my elbow, see—"

No sooner had they closed the attic door when they heard Mrs. Allbright holler from the bottom step.

"We have to go to the city tomorrow to visit our grandparents," said Dillon tonelessly, dragging his feet down the stairway. "But we'll be home after dinner. Let's meet then, okay?"

"Sounds great," said Kipper excitedly, looking at the others, who nodded. "See you then."

Dillon and Sarina shivered in the cool air as they watched their friends disappear down the dark drive. It was so different from the city. No slamming car doors, yelling in the streets, or drunken bums breaking whiskey bottles on the pavement. Windy Drive was so quiet all you heard were the crickets. Even the stars in the indigo sky seemed brighter. But the mystical scenes Dillon had witnessed lately told him things were about to change.

CHAPTER SIX

THE INVITATION

Dillon twisted and turned in bed. He couldn't stop thinking about the mysterious note. The house was dead as a graveyard, except for Dr. Allbright's snores echoing from the other end of the hall.

It was exactly midnight. Dillon sprang off the bed, reached for his glasses, and switched on his desk lamp. He sat quietly, replaying the contents of the note in his head.

Moments later, he snatched a piece of paper from his private stationery, along with a very short pencil. Remembering the words by heart, he quickly jotted:

It's not what it appears. My walls have ears.
If you should find this note at night,
make sure the moon is full delight.

"What could this mean?" he said to himself, drumming the first sentence with the pencil.

A sudden idea illuminated his brain. Heart thudding, he leapt up. "That's it!" Luckily, nobody heard him through all the noise from his father's snoring.

"*It's not what it appears,*" he whispered, sitting again. "That means something's fake, like an illusion. Something in that attic isn't real. But what?"

Dillon bit down on the pencil, indenting another notch. He focused his thoughts like a laser beam, knowing a solution was forthcoming.

"An illusion . . . an illusion," he repeated. He paused, and then said, "It must mean that the walls or ceiling are an illusion. But it doesn't make sense."

He began tapping the desk, until his strained eyes widened. A piece of the puzzle unraveled, and the mystery of the note began to unfold. "It isn't logical, unless . . . there's space behind it," he whispered to himself, tossing the pencil onto the desk.

Dillon closed his eyes, recalling the external appearance of the house. He clearly saw the many peaks of the roof. One section sprouted to a point. There were definitely two round windows at the top. But inside, the attic only had one.

Dillon stared straight ahead, unable to think another thought. He was convinced he'd cracked the mystery of the note. He desperately wanted to wake Sarina, but it was one-thirty.

It was only when he was back in bed that it struck Dillon that he wouldn't be able to tell his friends until he'd returned from the city. He would have to wait a whole day. Exhausted, Dillon sank into his pillow and drifted off into a deep sleep.

The disturbing dreams of the previous night reentered his sleep. But this time, he was an active participant. He vividly saw himself sword fighting with a husky, dark figure. He strained to see the warrior's face, but it was no use.

Pinned against a stone wall, he felt the swift sharpness of a blade rip through his right forearm. He screamed in agony as the blood stained his shirt. There was a laugh, the most horrendous laugh Dillon had ever heard. It was filled with an indescribable evil he'd never felt before. He wanted desperately to wake from this nightmare, but the duel played on, taunting his very soul.

"Stop laughing," Dillon mumbled as the screeching grew louder in his ear. "Quit it . . . go away . . ."

Dillon's eyes opened. He found himself covered in sweat. He wished he could forget his dream, but he couldn't. The moon was gleaming through the window. And something was gawking at him. A black, feathered, long-beaked something.

Sir Duke was perched outside Dillon's window.

*   ☀   *

"*Sir Duke!*" whispered Dillon breathlessly, bolting to the window and lifting it up. "What are you doing here?" He noticed a crumpled paper hanging from the bird's beak. Suddenly, a bossy voice spoke in his head.

"Well, what are you waiting for? I don't have all night!"

Dillon gasped.

He jerked his head around the room but realized he was alone. He must have heard the raven's voice telepathically, he thought. Lady Norton was right—telepathy really did work.

"Hello-o-o. The least you can do is take the paper."

"Are . . . are you talking to *me*?" faltered Dillon. "I can't believe it. I can hear you in my head." Dillon reached out and gently removed the folded paper. A gob of drool dribbled from Sir Duke's beak.

Dillon listened, but there was nothing except snoring from the hallway. He turned to Sir Duke, who fell silent, and then opened the note at once. It said, in an emerald-green scribble:

Dear Dillon,
Meet me at my shack at three.
But first, you must listen to Sir Duke carefully.
See you soon!
Lady Norton

Dillon's heart pounded. He couldn't figure out why Lady Norton wanted to meet so early in the morning. He looked up at Sir Duke and murmured, "She wants to talk to *me*?"

Sir Duke's beak seemed to wrinkle in a grin. The raven instructed Dillon to lie on the bed with his eyes closed. Dillon thought this was an odd request. After all, if he fell asleep, he'd miss his appointment. He was intending to sneak outside and get his bike from the garage.

"Good heavens, boy." Sir Duke's eyes rolled. "You really thought you'd travel the *long* way?"

Dillon didn't realize his thoughts penetrated the raven's head. It was plain that whatever conversation they had, it was spoken without a voice box. Exactly how it happened was a mystery to Dillon, but he continued the conversation in his head. "Well, I . . ."

"There's no need for physical transportation," Sir Duke reassured him. "Listen carefully. I do believe you'll love this one!"

Dillon nodded.

He was beginning to trust his feathered friend and knew he was in safe hands. Sir Duke repeated the instructions. Dillon was to lie on the bed with his eyes closed and focus on his breathing. He was to take ten deep breaths. On each exhale, he'd feel his muscles relax, releasing any stored tensions.

Since it was early morning, this was easy for Dillon. He was already sleepy. Sir Duke spoke in a hypnotic tone, making him feel even more relaxed. Dillon's breathing became deep and even. He felt his entire body sink into the bed, bringing him deeper and deeper.

". . . now visualize a white light surrounding your body; this is your protective shield. You're feeling peaceful now, going further and further inward . . ."

Dillon awoke as if shaken out of a dream. Where was he? Then he remembered. He saw Sir Duke sitting on the windowsill. It was still dark. Things were fuzzy, like he was looking through a dirty window. He'd placed his glasses on the nightstand . . . yes, that would explain the fuzziness, but why did he feel so light-headed? Whatever Sir Duke had intended to do, it hadn't worked. He was still in his room.

"What happened?" Dillon asked Sir Duke as he found himself gliding over to the window. "I must have drifted off. What time is it?" He felt sluggish as his body swayed with the rhythm of the night.

"We're right on schedule, my boy. Shall we go? As I say, I'll take the lead . . ."

Dillon was confused. Go where? He wanted to check his clock. He turned to his bed, but instead, his eyes fell on someone lying on it.

Dillon tried not to shout, but it was hard not to. Who was sleeping on his bed? The moment he thought it, he found himself standing, no, *hovering* over the bed. For a second, Dillon didn't realize what was happening. And then he saw.

"It couldn't be," he told himself.

Dillon was looking at himself. It was *his* body lying there!

As he stared down at himself tangled in the covers, he heard Sir Duke's comforting voice say, "No, you're not dead. You're in your astral body. Isn't it invigorating?"

Dillon wasn't sure what the raven was talking about, but it didn't matter. Some explanations confused him. He couldn't explain the out-of-body experience, nor deny it. No, there were no words to describe what he truly felt.

Dillon was shimmery, of course, but no different from his solid body lying still on the bed. His features were the same, like a duplicate had been made of his body.

He swooped down effortlessly, snatched his glasses, and glanced at the clock. It was quarter to three. He didn't want to be late for his first official meeting, so he better hurry. Next thing he knew, he was floating by the window.

The bird and boy gazed excitedly into each other's eyes. Dillon had no trouble digesting the experience. He'd always dreamed of flying. Sir Duke's beak formed into a smile, and then he fluttered off into the night air.

Dillon took one last glance at the bed. To his amazement, his other body was bathed in a bright light. It glowed in the darkened room. He whispered, "I'll be back soon." He knew, somehow, what to do. He turned in midair and glided out the window.

The roof of the house fell away, dropping out of sight as his light body soared above the treetops. The clear, dark sky blossomed with stars, and the moon cast an unreal light over Windy Drive. A breeze brushed through his hair and whistled in his ears. The glistening lawns of Willow Creek lay silent below him.

Dillon's body expanded in a jolt of excitement. For the first time in his life, he was free as a bird. Dillon flew through the neighborhood, down side streets, and through deserted gardens.

Harriet Wimple's bed sat against the window, and since the moon was bright, it shone on her pillow and awakened her. Lying groggily in her night curlers, Harriet happened to turn when Dillon swept past. A quivering flash, wearing glasses, was gone before she could call anyone. Harriet rubbed her eyes and fell back into a restless sleep.

Dillon caught a glimpse of Oak Tree Road. He'd pay a visit to Tommy and Tara's house. He flew past the signpost, confident his body would lead the way.

The moon reflected off the windows of a ruddy house with layers of peeling paint. An eerie silence drifted off a graveyard—no, it was something else. Dillon swooped down over a grassy field of over-turned mowers, blown tires, and broken cars. There was no doubt. Dillon had found the Flick's house.

Dillon wondered were Kipper lived, and before he knew it, he was skimming the treetops. He heard a dog barking in the distance. He made a sudden dip and found himself hovering over a rusty mailbox. It read, "The Reeves, No. 218 Steeplechase Lane."

Kipper's house wasn't what he'd expected. It was wonderful. Dillon's eyes glinted behind his glasses as he floated down the dirt lane toward number 218.

The old house stood by itself at the bottom of the hill. A modest orchard full of plump apples was reflected in the moonlight, and the tips of grass sparkled with dew. Dillon squinted down at a small gar-den overflowing with tomato plants and fresh vegetables. The sound of bullfrogs from a nearby pond croaked in his ears.

He drifted before the still house. The dark windows showed no sign of movement. He wanted to find Kipper's bedroom window. Obeying his command, his body flew to the back of the house.

Dillon hovered over a thick branch and peered through a window. Kipper Reeves was sleeping soundly. "See you later," Dillon whis-pered. He zoomed up over the branches and up past the chimney. Kipper's house shrank beneath him as he flew toward Main Street.

Flying gracefully out of town, Dillon spotted the silhouette of Sir Duke.

In an unexpected burst, Dillon sped closer with his glasses press-ing tight to his face. He glanced back. Willow Creek was a blur, and to his surprise, he was flying alongside the raven.

Sir Duke glanced over and said nonchalantly, "It's jolly well time you caught up!"

Dillon was totally immersed in the moment. He never knew how *real* his thoughts were, until now. Whenever he thought of a place to be or someone to see—BAM! He could be there in an instant. He couldn't wait to get home to write a list of exotic places to visit like . . . Hawaii . . . or Aruba. Before, it wasn't possible, but now . . .

They flew over a clump of trees. Only the glinting lights behind told them a town was not far away. Sir Duke flew low, skimming the dark branches. He made a sudden dip and disappeared into the leaves. Dillon followed closely behind.

A ray of moonlight lit the branches above. Sir Duke dropped lower and flew toward open ground. Dillon squinted through the darkness for a landing spot.

Soon after, he burst into a blaze of moonlight and landed smoothly on a clump of pearly grass. Dillon stood silently in the shadow of Lady Norton's shack.

Its dingy windows twinkled with the reflection of the starry sky. In his mind's eye, he saw Lady Norton sitting by a fireplace, waiting patiently for them, sipping a cup of piping-hot tea, a white candle burning on the mantle . . .

"At last, my boy!" Sir Duke flew over to the door and squawked loudly. "A marvelous trip! I say, it's delightful to have company!"

The door swung open, and the plump body of Lady Norton appeared in the doorway. Sir Duke flew to her shoulder.

Dillon heard a familiar voice: "I see you've arrived on time," said Lady Norton with a smile. "Pleased you could make it. Do come in."

Dillon was intrigued. She could *see* him. Although he was a phantom at the moment, Lady Norton treated him no differently. Dillon glided happily through the front door.

There were three rooms inside. Dried flowers hung from a rafter, crystals sparkled everywhere, a kettle was boiling over the fireplace, and burning brightly on the mantle was a white candle.

Dillon smiled. The vivid picture in his head had been correct.

"Join me by the fire, Dillon," said Lady Norton, who was pouring boiling water over a sweet-smelling tea bag. "I'm very partial to herbal teas. Did you enjoy your trip?"

Dillon nodded and then glided over.

Meanwhile, Sir Duke sat quietly with his eyes closed, looking like he was resting.

"I'd offer you some, but I'm afraid it'll go right through you," Lady Norton said, chuckling as she glanced at Dillon's shimmering body. "Astrotraveling is quite fun, once you get the hang of it. It comes in handy for late night meetings—nobody can see you . . . well, except people like me." Lady Norton winked.

Dillon felt happy to be there. "Thanks for inviting me," he said reverently. "I have been meaning to speak with you."

"Ah—the feeling was mutual. I have something to discuss with you. It's about your . . . *gift*." Her eyes twinkled in the firelight.

Sir Duke's eyes opened. He shifted on Lady Norton's shoulder, looking like he was suddenly interested in their conversation.

Dillon was surprised. How did Lady Norton know about his unique abilities? He couldn't imagine where she'd gotten the information. Dillon knew they heard his thoughts—his voice repeated off the walls. There was no privacy in an astral body, he thought.

Lady Norton just smiled knowingly. "No need to concern yourself," she said cheerfully. "I'm here to help." She reached for her piping-hot cup and took a sip of tea.

Dillon's body expanded. He glided over to a vacant chair that sat across from Lady Norton and hovered gingerly in the seat. "Nobody ever explained things before. My parents never believe me. Kids at school tease me and teachers give me dirty looks." As Dillon lowered his head, his light dimmed.

After what seemed a long while, Lady Norton spoke.

"Yes, yes, some people are like that," she said sadly, placing her cup down. "They're afraid of things they don't understand. Most unfortunately, this kind of behavior suppresses the gifted one. Children like yourself start doubting their extrasensory capabilities." Lady Norton peered at Dillon. "But we mustn't grumble. It does us no good."

Dillon nodded.

"Ain't that the truth," said Sir Duke suddenly. "If you ask me—"

"Shush," whispered Lady Norton.

Sir Duke ruffled his feathers and flew across the small room. He landed on a windowsill with his back turned. Dillon heard him say, "Well!"

After giving the raven a displeased look, Lady Norton continued. "Everyone can learn to play the violin, but not everyone can be a concert violinist, you see. We all have talents. Yours happens to be in the field of the paranormal. Your "gift" isn't for your benefit, Dillon. It's to help others." Lady Norton stood up, broke off a twig of sage, lit one end in the fire, and then placed it in a seashell, which was filled with ashes.

The smoke quickly enveloped the room. It captured heavy shadows hiding in corners and swallowed them whole. The room illuminated in a surrealistic glow.

Dillon heard a low, rhythmic toning. It was the trancelike sound of people chanting, but in a different language. Singing bowls and drumming merged into the continuous drone. What he heard was uplifting. It was everywhere. He glanced quickly at Lady Norton. But she was busy pouring another cup of tea.

Then something startling happened.

As Dillon stared dreamily into a billowy cloud, a bald head appeared, then a man's face. Dillon gasped when the eyes blinked opened. Somehow, Dillon knew it was a Tibetan monk. But why was the monk *here?*

The mouth opened in a warm smile, and a gentle voice spoke: "Your gift, as one might say, is your calling." The monk looked directly into Dillon's wide blue eyes.

It may have been only seconds, but to Dillon the moment was timeless. Instantly he felt a connection with this man whom he'd met only moments ago.

"I'm your spirit guide, Dillon," the monk said calmly. "I'm assigned to help with your work. Lady Norton will train you well." His eyes shifted to Lady Norton and then back to Dillon. "When the dove appears, we shall speak again." The monk blended with the smoke and vanished.

Dillon quickly turned to Lady Norton, who was nodding.

"Yes, you've met your master teacher. Not everyone can see their spirit guides, but that doesn't mean they aren't there. Let me see . . ." she said slowly, as if to herself. "We have much to do. Yes, lots of studying . . ." Lady Norton hummed as she added a small log to the fire.

Dillon watched the dancing flames lick the hearth walls. He'd been clueless how the meeting would unfold. But it was clear he'd discovered his life's purpose.

It would explain why Dillon couldn't see his future, but could predict the futures of others with validating confirmation. A few years ago, he'd done "readings" for family and relatives. They'd often say, "How could you know—you weren't even born yet." He recalled being thrilled when he located the neighbor's missing dog and found his father's keys. Dillon stared into the core of a wild flame, where a brilliant blue light flickered alone, and vowed to never doubt himself again.

Dillon Allbright was being prepared for an extraordinary future. If he were told prematurely what was to come, the responsibility would have overwhelmed him. Lady Norton's encouraging words were like food to his spirit. He was eager to soak up more of the world of psychic phenomena.

It was agreed they'd meet every Friday at midnight. Dillon would be trained in metaphysical and alchemical philosophies, numerology, astrology, palmistry, dowsing, rune stones, and tarot cards. He'd receive a sound understanding of psychic energy, meditation, and yoga. He'd practice seeing auras, and, according to the color surrounding the person, he'd determine their frame of mind. And he'd learn his weaknesses and fine-tune his strengths.

That memorable evening, Lady Norton told Dillon of unique psychics who had helped police solve the most horrendous crimes. He learned of people who used their gifts to heal others. He learned of animal and plant communicators. The more Dillon heard, the more he knew he was on his path.

Lady Norton yawned. "Oh, dear," she said abruptly, looking distressed. She stood up at once. "It's five in the morning, and you're visiting your grandparents today—"

"Oh, Miss Norton," Dillon stared around the room, "must I leave so soon?"

"I'm afraid so," said Lady Norton, trying to balance herself on a stepladder. She carefully leaned forward and blew out the white candle. "Now remember next Friday."

"Yes, but . . ." said Dillon grimly, "it's just . . ."

"Your *gift*—yes, you'll know what to do when the time comes, dear. Well, now, off you go." She turned suddenly. "Oh, a word of warning. If you misuse your gift for selfish purposes—it can be taken away, you see." Her eyes narrowed.

Dillon nodded.

He turned to say goodbye to Sir Duke, but the raven was snoring. He turned back again, and Lady Norton was gone. Instead, he was looking at a closed bedroom door. Dillon felt exhausted. He'd forgotten to tell Lady Norton about the mysterious note from the attic. His body felt heavy, and his eyes kept closing.

Lady Norton's voice spoke suddenly in his head.

"Oh, I forgot your assignment. Better listen carefully, dear. Since your family moved here, the population number has been changed on the town's signpost. I find the number very magical. What's the meaning of the *new* number? Ponder over it and have the answer by next Friday."

"*Population* number?" Dillon said sluggishly, wishing he was home in bed.

The room fell away, and Dillon Allbright slipped into nothingness.

CHAPTER SEVEN

THE MAN IN THE SILVER CLOAK

Dillon woke with a start. He found himself lying in his bed. He tried to remember the dream he'd been having. It was really strange. He was flying with Sir Duke to Lady Norton's shack. It seemed so real. Lady Norton was talking to him about his *gift* . . . a Tibetan monk appeared in a cloud of smoke . . . he spoke of his *calling* . . .

Suddenly, Dillon felt wide-awake. A delicious smell of frying bacon was wafting from the griddle. His stomach rumbled with hunger. He sprang up, and the message on the portrait popped into his head. Excitement flooded through him. He couldn't wait to tell Sarina his idea.

He slid in his floppy socks to Sarina's bedroom, but to his disappointment, her bed was neatly made and the room was vacant. At that moment, he heard Sarina's voice coming from downstairs. He caught a few words of what she was saying.

"Mom, are we leaving, yet—?"

There were footsteps and then a deep voice.

"Dillon!" shouted Dr. Allbright, standing in the doorway. "What are you doing? Get a move on, son. We'll be leaving soon."

Dillon stumbled backward at once. "I was just—"

"Come along, now." Dr. Allbright snatched his shoulder and

pushed him out the door. "Go get dressed. Your mother made—breakfast," he said with an outburst of dry coughs.

Dr. Allbright looked as though he had swallowed something that made him sick.

Dillon saw a vision of his mother cooking. She was serving runny eggs. Dillon tried not to laugh as he walked back to his room. He heard his father hack all the way down the hall.

Dillon found his jeans lying on the floor and, after yanking them on, felt in his pockets. Every time they were in the city, his parents stopped at Barnes & Noble. Dillon wished he could spend the whole day there. The bookstore was huge, and he'd wander over to the kids' section to buy himself the hottest fiction.

"Dillon!" called Mrs. Allbright from the foot of the steps. "Breakfast is ready!"

"I'll be right there, Mom!"

Dillon heard her walking toward the kitchen. He pulled out his allowance money to see what was left. To his surprise, a wrinkled note was stuffed between a five and ten dollar bill. It read:

Dear Dillon,
Meet me at my shack at three.
But first, you must listen to Sir Duke carefully.
See you soon!
Lady Norton

Dillon's eyes bulged. The memory of what had happened hit him. I *was* flying with Sir Duke! He went straight to the window, lifted it open, and hung his head outside. Although the raven wasn't there, Lady Norton's note was enough to prove it had really happened.

Dillon's mind raced. Should he tell Sarina and his best friend, Kipper? Something held him back. It would be a difficult story to believe. He ripped the note into tiny pieces and discarded it in the garbage pail. For the first time, Dillon decided to keep a secret to himself.

During breakfast, Dillon tried kicking Sarina's leg under the table, but swiped her knee by accident. She threw him a dirty look. He just had to tell her about Fickle's note and how he'd figured out a piece of the puzzle. He tried motioning to her from across the table, but caught his mother's eye instead.

Not long ago, Dillon had invented his very own sign language. Unfortunately, his sister didn't understand his silly hand gestures and his ridiculous facial expressions, so she ignored him.

One expression that seemed to annoy her was when Dillon puckered his cheeks like a blowfish, or was it a balloon? To Dillon, it meant he'd burst if he didn't tell his latest idea. Mrs. Allbright happened to look up again and caught him in the act.

"What *are* you doing?"

"Nothing," said Dillon. He bent his face over his plate and shoveled in a mouthful of food.

Dr. Allbright, meanwhile, drank his coffee and ate his wife's gooey eggs. Mrs. Allbright's lips pursed when he tried to sneak five slices of bread.

* ❂✳ *

The clock ticked slowly as Dillon counted the day away. He'd bought *Bed-Knob and Broomstick* by Mary Norton and was already on the sixth chapter. "You've got to get it—it's a classic," a bright-eyed kid had told him.

Dillon hadn't had a chance to speak to Sarina because his grandparents kept her occupied. When his eyes were strained from reading, he allowed himself to think of the message on the portrait. If his theory was correct, the attic was an illusion, and Fickle's smirking portrait was the first clue of where to begin.

At nightfall, the Allbrights approached the dilapidated sign welcoming them to Willow Creek. Four more citizens had been added. It now read, "Population 1,618."

Sir Duke sat perched on the sign as if he were awaiting their return. Dillon smiled at the raven as they drove by. He heard Sir Duke's voice in his inner ear say, "It's jolly well time you're back, my boy! Better not forget your assignment!"

Dillon was confused. His *assignment?*

Then he remembered Lady Norton's words: "What's the meaning of the *new* number?" When he repeated the number 1,618 in his head, he kept seeing a golden circle. How could a circle have anything to do with it? Dillon strained his memory of geometry, but nothing came to mind. He felt frustrated and decided he'd think of the solution later.

Willow Creek appeared normal, except for a commotion at the town hall. The people looked agitated, chattering rapidly to one another.

A large group was gathered at the front doors, absorbed in conversation. When Dr. Allbright pulled the car over, Dillon caught a few words in his psychic ear. "That's what I saw!" gasped Jake Driblet. "I saw the same thing!" cried Bessie Beetle. (Driblet owned Jake's Hardware Store and Beetle owned Bessie's Antique Shop.)

Also standing there were Dr. Hearty, George McNulty, Ralph Picit, Harriet Wimple, Smitty, and Homer Bumpkin, the mayor. It was obvious something important was taking place.

Dr. Allbright stuck his head out the window, and his eyes fell on Dr. Hearty, who was standing close by. When Dr. Hearty spotted him, he waved him over.

"Trudy, you stay with the kids." Dr. Allbright stepped out of the car. "I'll just be a minute."

Dr. Allbright hadn't gotten halfway when Dr. Hearty grabbed his arm. "D-Did you hear what happened, Norman?" Dr. Hearty tilted his head to peer at the Allbright's car. He shot a fake smile at Mrs. Allbright, gave a floppy wave to the kids, and then looked back at Dr. Allbright. "I didn't want to believe it."

Dr. Hearty looked shaken, Wimple quivered, and Smitty chain-smoked. Beetle talked quickly to Driblet, while McNulty and Picit paced the sidewalk. The other folks argued with the harassed-looking Bumpkin.

Overwhelmed with curiosity, Mrs. Allbright and the kids sprinted from the car and joined Dr. Allbright, who looked not at all happy to see them. He spoke to Dr. Hearty as if they weren't there. Dillon listened intently to the conversation.

"We've been out of town, Rufeous. What's going on?"

Dr. Hearty stroked his bushy mustache and told Dr. Allbright what he'd heard from Harriet Wimple. "Around six, Harriet was driving past Windy Drive. A strange gentleman stood by the signpost, talking to a raven . . . well, that's what she thinks she saw." Dr. Hearty shook his head. "He was dressed in this silver cloak with these large green buttons. His white beard hung below his waist. She can't forget his bright eyes—they made her extremely nervous." Dr. Hearty kept looking behind his back.

Dillon's blue eyes bulged. *A man in a silver cloak?* Was it the man in his vision? A wave of anxiety made his heart race. He'd have to say something.

"Um, Dad," he muttered nervously, leaning close to his father. "I have to tell you something—"

"Not now, Dillon," Dr. Allbright said sharply, shooting him a look.

"But, this is important . . ."

Dr. Allbright ignored him. His son was known to be impulsive—everything seemed important. Dillon would delve into a project without thinking, which annoyed Dr. Allbright. Dillon had agreed some of his ideas were disastrous. "At least I'm not afraid to try something different," he'd told his father hotly. Dillon was the type to take action, while others watched.

Dillon didn't say another word as his father continued speaking with Dr. Hearty.

"Perhaps he was passing through town, heading toward the city to a costume party. Really, Rufeous, is this what the fuss is about?"

"Goodness no, Norman." Dr. Hearty's eyes twitched uncontrollably. "You didn't give me time to finish my story."

"All right then," mumbled Dr. Allbright. "Please, carry on."

Dr. Hearty sighed heavily and then continued. "After Harriet had driven past this peculiar gentleman, she watched him in her mirror, but he was gone. She jerked her head around and saw nobody, not even the raven. Harriet quickly turned her car around, assuming he was walking up *your* street, but he was nowhere in sight."

"I'm sure there's a logical explanation," said Dr. Allbright in an unconvinced tone.

"That's not all. Jake Driblet's saying he saw the same gentleman standing outside his store, which is on the opposite side of town, and the man was dressed in a silver cloak. It happened at six, which was when Harriet saw him. And we both know it takes some time to walk across town. How do you like that, Norman?" Dr. Hearty took a small case from his pocket, shook out two pink pills with his trembling hand, and popped them in his mouth.

Dr. Allbright acted uninterested and said, "I'm sure there's some reason, Rufeous."

Dillon heard his father's deepest thoughts in his psychic ear. It revealed Dr. Allbright's true feelings. There must be some logic to this story, Dr. Allbright thought. But nobody could be at two places at once. Who was this strange man, and what was his business in Willow Creek? He was obviously lost. Yes, that would be it.

A few minutes later, McNulty and Picit dashed over.

"G-G-Good evening, Norman," McNulty sputtered, spraying Dr. Allbright's face. "Did you h-hear the story? I've been here sixty-one years and have never seen such rubbish! I was paying no mind, pulling weeds from behind the firehouse, when, j-jumping jellybeans, an old feller was standing beside me!" McNulty jumped back a few feet and almost fell over.

It took a few seconds before McNulty could continue. It was as though his brain had trouble retrieving the memory. Dr. Allbright leaned forward and took a sniff.

"He was an odd-looking chap, dressed in this silver cloak with these funny buttons. I got myself up, and the feller was gone. Just like that, he vanished before me," said McNulty, trying to snap his fingers together, but missing. "I was about to have my noggin examined, when Ralph Picit told me he'd seen the feller, too."

Picit nodded at Dr. Allbright, who was beginning to look perplexed.

"About what time did you see this old gentleman, George," asked Dr. Allbright curiously.

"Wait a minute now, let me see," said McNulty, thinking so hard his forehead wrinkled. "Ah, yes, now I remember, it was six on the nose—"

"That's when I saw the white-bearded man at the back of the post office," chimed in Picit. "He sure gave me the willies. He had this suspicious-looking smile." Picit shuttered. "I figured he was thinking of robbing me."

The four men looked at each other. The blood drained from Dr. Allbright's face. He found it humorous to hear a tale from McNulty, but not from sober people. How could this mysterious stranger be at so many places at once? Something weird was going on, and they all wanted to get to the bottom of it. Finally, Mayor Bumpkin spoke a few words.

"Settle down now, everyone! Settle down!" Bumpkin was tiny and looked like a weasel in a pinstriped suit. "I can assure you by tomorrow morning, we'll get to the bottom of this! So tonight, for your safety, Smitty will be on patrol! Go back to your homes!" he squeaked. "We have everything under control—"

A strong gale disrupted Bumpkin's speech. Wimple's straw hat blew clear off her orange beehive head of hair. Smitty's cigarette went out, and Dr. Hearty's bushy mustache fluttered against his fat face. For some unknown reason, the gust of wind appeared only at the town hall.

Rumbles of thunder shook the earth. It overrode the howl of the wind. It grew steadily louder as they looked up at the sky. They couldn't help noticing that someone was standing on the town hall roof.

"Look!" shouted Wimple, pointing up with a shaky finger. "It's *him*—that's the man I saw!"

The silver-cloaked man's long beard whipped in the wind. His legs looked like tree trunks that were deeply rooted to the shingles. He somehow remained steady, even though the wind was intensely strong. The mysterious man launched into a speech.

"Hear ye, people of Willow Creek!" he declared, while the wind swept his cloak. "It's a time of celebration!" His face was bright, and his hand swayed in harmony with his words. "Tonight is the opening of the seal!"

The listeners' mouths hung open. Dillon wanted to run but couldn't move his legs. He stood trembling, eyeing the man closely. "What did he mean by 'the opening of the seal?'" he asked his mother. But Mrs. Allbright couldn't speak. "Mom, are you okay?"

"There's no need for fear, my dear people!" shouted the man. "I've come in peace!" His wild eyes beamed down at them.

Everyone gasped when the man drew a brilliant sword from underneath his cloak and raised it high in the air. An emerald-green star was embedded in the massive handle. It pulsated a green glow against the inky sky.

Dillon recognized the sword from his vision and in the bathtub.

Fear traveled through his veins. He was face-to-face with the man who had stolen Fickle's package and possibly killed him. Dillon glanced over at Sarina, but she didn't seem to notice him. The pasty look on her face told him she was terrified.

A sudden pain seared Dillon's right forearm. He gasped. A long cut, deep enough for stitches, oozed with blood, soaking the pavement. He felt nauseous as he tried hiding the spill with his sneaker, but it was no use.

The frightening scene faded in and out. Before Dillon's eyes, the cut healed and the pain subsided. Dillon wondered. Was it the same wound he'd received in his nightmare? Why hadn't anyone else seen the pool of blood? People were standing all around him. It must have been an illusion, but all the same, the pain . . .

Dillon almost told his father but changed his mind. He glanced down at his healed arm, thinking . . . no, he couldn't tell anyone. He didn't want to cause more worry; they were upset enough.

The crowd backed into each other. Dr. Hearty turned a shade of green. Wimple clapped her hands to her mouth, and Smitty clutched his holstered gun. Dillon couldn't blame him. He figured Smitty wasn't taking any chances.

As fast as the wind came up, it settled down. The man's strong right hand held his sword high, while the other clutched his cloak. He bowed toward the silent crowd and smiled. His twinkling eyes flashed in the direction of Dillon.

Was the stranger looking at *him?*

Instantly, as if to answer his question, Dillon heard a deep voice in his head say, "Yes, Dillon, I was looking at you." It seemed the voice only existed in his head; everyone else looked preoccupied with fear.

A horrifying thought struck Dillon. Was the stranger psychic, too? What if the man knew where he lived? Before Dillon could think of anything else—before another thought invaded his mind—the silver-cloaked man disappeared mysteriously into the night sky.

Who was this silver-cloaked man, and what did he want with Willow Creek? What did he mean about the opening of the seal?

And where, when, and how would it be opened?

Mayor Bumpkin promised he'd do everything in his power to resolve this disturbance. The townsfolk whispered to each other as they hurried back to the safety of their homes. Nobody noticed Sir Duke flutter past a nearby lamppost. If they had, they might have thought it was the same raven that had conversed with the silver-cloaked man, or was it?

Dr. Hearty looked enraged as he scurried along with McNulty and Picit. What would the city media say if word got out about this disrupting incident? The nerve of this man showing up uninvited, blabbering nonsense from atop the roof!

Everything used to be normal and safe in Willow Creek. Now they weren't so sure. Dr. Allbright escorted his family back to the car. He looked anxious to get home and forget the whole matter.

A calmness stilled the evening air. Nobody knew what to expect next, but there was no doubt something unusual was happening. Ever since the Allbrights moved to Willow Creek, there had been reports of wind squalls and lightning on the hill of Windy Drive. Experts had been unable to explain or predict its erratic weather patterns.

CHAPTER EIGHT

FICKLE'S FULL MOON

When the Allbrights turned up Windy Drive, they saw a group of kids huddled in front of the gated entryway to their home. It appeared they'd been waiting for quite some time, because they were sitting on the pavement engrossed in conversation.

"That's Kipper and the gang!" cried Dillon, hanging over the front seat. "Look, Sarina!"

"Why are your friends here again?" asked Mrs. Allbright curiously, turning in her seat.

"Oh, Mom," muttered Dillon. "They won't stay late, I promise."

Trudy Allbright knew her son was up to something. Although not psychic herself, Dillon's "weirdness" was taken for granted in their house. Her son was most likely giving private readings again.

On the other hand, after what Dr. Allbright had just witnessed, the kids looked like angels.

The kids parted, whispering fervently to each other. Dr. Allbright pressed a remote button on his visor, opening the gates. Dillon and Sarina watched anxiously through the back window as their friends followed behind the family car.

Everyone greeted each other by the stone steps.

"Good evening, Mr. and Mrs. Allbright," said Kipper. "Sure is a beautiful evening, isn't it?"

"Why yes . . . yes, it is young man," answered Dr. Allbright happily, nudging his wife in the arm. "Isn't it Trudy?"

"Yes . . . yes it is," sputtered Mrs. Allbright, looking at the children.

For a few uncomfortable minutes, everyone stood in silence, until Kipper spoke.

"Have you heard the story about Henry Fickle?" he asked, looking wide-eyed at Mr. and Mrs. Allbright.

Mr. and Mrs. Allbright glanced at each other. Although they'd heard the rumor from Harriet Wimple, they seemed to not want to disappoint the boy. After all, he looked anxious to tell his story.

It was one of those moments when the expanded story was even more eerie than the original one. Everyone listened with great interest, while Dillon sighed deeply. Kipper told the Allbrights everything he'd heard, plus a new version. When Kipper told them, quite seriously, he'd seen a spaceship and that Fickle was taken away by aliens, Tara and Sarina gasped. Thanks to Kipper Reeves, the story of Henry Fickle got better each time.

Dillon began fidgeting in his pockets. He stared off into the evening sky, allowing his eyes to roam over the top of the house. He caught a glimpse of the full moon—and *two* round windows.

Dillon had trouble containing his excitement. "Well, we're going inside," he said casually, sneaking a wink at the others. He had to drag Kipper away; he seemed to want to stay.

Mr. and Mrs. Allbright were left standing alone. During the brief conversation, Dr. Allbright appeared to have gotten a grip on himself. He sat down on the damp steps, admiring the view below. "Ah, Trudy, dear," he said joyously. "This sure is the life. No more rush hour traffic to contend with or waiting in long lines."

Mrs. Allbright plopped down next to her husband and thought, no more shopping at her favorite stores, name-brand outlets, or dining at exquisite restaurants. No, she'd be shopping in town, wearing the same clothes as everyone else, dining at Betty Lou's Kitchen on sandwich platters with a pickle, coleslaw, and a bag of chips.

Sir Duke fluttered out of a nearby pine tree, startling Mrs. Allbright. The raven was in the area again, most likely catching the latest gossip. He must have followed them home, flying unseen above their car.

* ❧ ✸ ☾ *

The kids sat in a circle on Dillon's bedroom floor. Dillon was acting really weird, mumbling words to himself and pacing around the room.

"What's the matter?" Kipper asked, looking up at him.

Dillon placed his index finger over his mouth, telling everyone to be still. He tiptoed over to the door, pressed his ear against the wood, and cracked it open. After peering down both ends of the hall, he clicked the door shut.

"Last night," he said in a low-but-excited voice. "I figured out an important part of the note." He flopped down, taking a deep breath. He'd finally released his stored-up news.

They gazed unbelievingly at him. Now his sister could understand why he'd been trying to get her attention all day.

"I'm sorry, Dillon." She gently touched his arm. "I didn't know—"

WHACK!

Kipper smacked Dillon across the back, knocking his glasses off. "Well done! This kid is a genius! Just give him time, and he'll solve the mystery!" Kipper's face shone with admiration.

Dillon felt the heat rush to his face. He reached for his glasses and pushed them up his nose.

"Tell us about the note," said Tara at once, smiling proudly at him.

"Yeah," added Tommy, leaning in to listen. "What did you figure out?"

Dillon kneeled on both knees and placed his doodled paper on the floor. He told them Fickle's carefully chosen words were actually a set of instructions. He took pleasure in pointing to each sentence and explaining his findings.

"Let's start with the first sentence. I've concluded the walls or ceiling in the attic are fake. I believe behind one of them the laboratory's concealed." He looked up anxiously.

Nobody said a word, but Dillon was pleased to hear silence. It meant he'd captured their interest. Dillon was more than happy to continue.

"I analyzed an upper section of the roof and discovered two round windows on the outside. They're located one above the other. However, there's only *one* on the inside of the attic. So there's obviously another room."

Slowly, wonderingly, grins of delight formed across their faces.

"A room must be *above* the attic," Tommy said indignantly, looking up, "because below are these bedrooms." He looked wide-eyed around the room.

Kipper chimed in, "It has to be one level up. I bet a whole week's pay from my paper route on it." He looked excitedly at the others.

"That's how I figured it to be," said Dillon, beaming at Kipper and Tommy. "It would solve the second sentence. 'My walls have ears' means there's another space to communicate in. Do you get it?" His blue eyes twinkled behind his glasses. "It means someone's standing behind or above, listening." The hairs on the back of Dillon's neck prickled. It indicated a ghost was present, but it hadn't showed itself, yet.

"But where does the moon fit in?" Sarina asked curiously.

Dillon shrugged. "Don't know—but it's full moon tonight."

"There's only one way to find out!" said Kipper, springing up.

Everyone gave their nodding approval.

* ☾✳☽ *

They hurried up the narrow steps and reached the familiar room with its single, round window. Fickle's portrait was still leaning against the post.

"We don't have much time," panted Dillon, pacing across the floor. "Look for something unusual." He tried forcing an image, but nothing came to mind, except the same golden circle he'd seen earlier. *What's the meaning of the new number*, Lady Norton had asked.

The boys tapped on the ceiling, dropping dust and debris to the floor, while the girls hunted for clues. By the looks on their eager faces, they could have been searching for a moneybag. They were very, very close.

But all the same, they found nothing.

"What are we doing wrong?" coughed Kipper. He was covered from head to toe with dust. "We searched every inch of this place."

"What were you saying about giving *us* your newspaper money?" sneered Tommy, looking hungrily at Kipper.

At first, Kipper seemed to ignore Tommy's statement, but then he said sharply, "I didn't shake on it!"

"I don't understand," said Dillon, wiping his glasses on his shirt. "I thought—"

Dillon's train of thought was severed. He was distracted by his sister standing on her tiptoes, looking out the round window. "The moon," Sarina said carelessly, "is so bright and lovely. It lights up the whole sky."

Dillon wondered. How could she be so calm, while he unraveled at the seams? She wasn't concerned about finding Fickle's laboratory—she was mesmerized by the moon. He stood in awe, watching her sway in a dreamy trance, until a great idea hit him. "Of course! Why didn't I think of that?"

Everyone stopped in their tracks.

"Don't you see!" he said breathlessly, pointing to the window. "We can't see the full moon inside with the lights on! Let's turn them off and see what happens!"

At that moment, Dillon swore he saw a shadow on the other side of the room, but when he turned a second time, it was gone. Dillon wondered if it was Fickle's ghost or something else.

"Dillon's right," said Kipper. "Someone hit the lights."

"Wait!" Tara cried in panic, grabbing Tommy's shirt. "There might be monsters or hairy spiders. I hate dark places." She checked both her arms. "Do my arms look red, Sarina?"

Sarina shook her head, while Tommy and Kipper rolled their eyes.

A grin spread over Dillon's face. "Don't worry," Dillon assured Tara. "The room will light up like a Christmas tree. What do you say?"

"Well, okay. But do you think—"

"Hit the lights, Allbright!" yelled Tommy and Kipper together.

Dillon bolted down the staircase and switched off the lights. He took a moment for his eyes to adjust. Moments later, a dull light appeared at the top steps. Excitement flooded through him as he raced back up. The entire room was bathed in light, and everyone was talking excitedly.

"Yes!" he said, dancing in the moonbeams. "I knew it would work!"

Then something caught Dillon's attention.

It was the golden circle, but this time a violet square was centered over it. The vivid image was painted on the walls, the ceiling, the floor—it was everywhere!

"Whoa-a-a!" breathed Dillon. "There must be hundreds of them!"

"What are you looking at, Dillon?" Kipper asked, looking blankly around the room.

"The golden circles—surely you see them?"

Kipper looked confused.

"Forget it, Kipper," Dillon muttered as he walked away. "It's nothing."

Dillon had forgotten about his psychic abilities. If the others had seen the circles, they would have mentioned it by now. Sometimes being psychic was a lonely profession, he thought.

Dillon lifted his head and saw Tara pointing breathlessly at the ceiling. She tried speaking, but no words would follow. Eventually, Dillon noticed what she was staring at.

A light sprinkled through the cracks of the ceiling boards, casting a pattern of long golden lines across the floor.

"There it is!" gasped Dillon. "It's Fickle's laboratory!"

The others quickly gathered, and everyone searched frantically for the entrance.

Something bright reflected off Dillon's glasses.

A light funneled through a small hole, projecting a symbol on a wooden post. Dillon's eyes fixed on interlocking, emerald-green triangles. But when he stood at an angle, it floated off the post into a three-dimensional star tetrahedron. Dillon's curious nature coaxed him to reach forward.

Instantly, his finger got zapped, like walking across a carpet in the wintertime. The shock wasn't strong enough to hurt him, but it was enough to spin the star tetrahedron counterclockwise.

As its speed increased, a human-sized, iridescent star tetrahedron appeared around his body. Before he could move, he found himself encased in a glass fluorescent tube. One end penetrated the apex of the tetrahedron and disappeared through the ceiling. The other end poked through the bottom of the tetrahedron and disappeared past his feet.

He quickly glanced at the others. To his surprise, they too, were held prisoner within their glass coffins. Neither of them had any idea what was happening; but one thing they knew for sure—they couldn't get out.

Dillon struggled, kicking and bouncing off his tubular wall. He looked helplessly around the room. What was happening? Was Kipper's spaceship story true? Were they held captive by some alien force?

So after getting this far, after figuring out the meaning of the note, after solving the mystery of the moon, and seeing a glimpse of the laboratory, they were going to die. Henry Fickle's portrait was probably smirking at how naïve they'd been. What would the townsfolk say when they discover five more people missing?

Dillon felt the tubes come alive, vibrating in a high-pitched hum like a field of tension wires. He realized it was over. A prayer would be in order, but before he'd gotten the words out, before he'd time to wave goodbye, a blinding flash filled the room.

The star tetrahedrons containing all five kids dissolved from sight. The room was left untouched, as though nobody had ever been there.

CHAPTER NINE

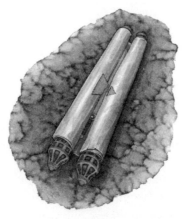

THE ANCIENT SCROLL

The attic was dissolving in a whirlpool of mixed colors, until it washed out of view. It was as if the children were everywhere, but nowhere. They were tiny particles spinning very fast. No thoughts came to mind. They just existed, still spinning and spinning.

Just when Dillon felt unbearably dizzy, the spacey experience stopped. The star tetrahedron and the tube were gone, but he felt disoriented and scared to move. He was alone but had no clue where he was. He noticed his body was transparent. Was he dead or having an out-of-body experience again?

He squinted around and spotted Tara. She looked thrilled to be no longer plump, but rather a thin mass of colored light.

Even though their bodies were made of light, they were able to recognize one another. Somehow, they'd maintained their identities and personalities. A mesh of color appeared before Dillon and Tara's eyes.

The others blinked into view. Their bodies were barely there, their minds only pulses of memory.

A translucent floor formed beneath their feet. As their bodies grew heavier and heavier, they found themselves standing solidly on a wooden floor. They were back to normal!

A room came into focus. It was dark except for a dull light filtering through a quarter of a cluttered window.

A wooden desk sat in front of them, and hanging over it was a picture. Tara couldn't help but notice a face peeking from behind a thick layer of spiderwebs. Behind them sat various pieces of furniture; another picture clung to the circular wall. All Dillon could see was people dressed in weird fashions, but no one in the frame was ever likely to be from Willow Creek.

To the left of the desk sat a circular bookcase with a third picture mounted above it. To the right, standing in the heavy shadows where the light scarcely reached its surface, was what looked like a long dining table.

"Where are we?" Sarina whispered to a wide outline standing next to her. "Is this heaven?"

"I think heaven's much brighter," answered Tara. "I sure hope this isn't . . . you know . . ."

A lurking feeling overtook the darkened room, waiting for the right moment to grab them.

Kipper ran his hands along the wall by the desk and then made a sudden turn around. "Don't just stand there!" he snapped. "Help me look for a light switch!"

The jumbled outlines came to life. Everyone felt their way around, except Tara. She was walking frantically about, mumbling to herself, when her head ran into something.

"Ouch!"

Tommy saw something swinging from the high ceiling. "What's that?" he asked, squinting. "It bonged against Tara's fat head." Tommy allowed himself a private laugh.

Dillon reached up and took hold of it. It was attached to a long wire that disappeared toward a pointed ceiling. A snapshot appeared in his mind's eye. "It's a work light," he said at once. "We have one in the garage."

Dillon got the impulse to check the wall opposite the desk. His heart lightened when his fingers touched a square metal plate. When he flipped the switch, the work light and various other fixtures illuminated the room.

"Who checked this wall before?" Dillon said with a grin, searching for Tommy. But Tara's voice ended his search.

"Look!" She pointed breathlessly to the dining table.

They were taken aback. The spectacular view wasn't a dining table—but a *laboratory* table!

The long table sat intertwined with a tangle of wire and tubing. Along its thick edges were outlets, knobs, and switches. A small sink overflowed with dirty bottles. And various beakers bubbled with colored fluids. One burped orange bubbles. Another released a green mist, and one puked a yellowish glob.

The laboratory appeared to be in operation, but nobody was there. Where was the unknown scientist?

"Well, I'll be," said Kipper, gazing at the table. "I wouldn't have believed it, myself."

"All this time," laughed Tommy, "we were standing in Fickle's laboratory."

Dillon stared blankly around the room, then drew a great shuddering breath and said, "The window!"

He scurried over to the circular bookcase and stood just to the right of the picture. He reached up, took a bunch of books that were sitting on a wide ledge, and placed them on the floor. The books had been covering most of the dirty window.

Before Dillon's wide eyes was the *second* round window. "I knew it!" He lowered his head. "We were transported here via the star tetrahedrons! They were the doorway in!" Dillon stood in awe. If he were able to predict everything, all the time, there'd be no element of surprise, he thought.

Fickle had designed a unique entryway. Who would think of an idea like that? Traveling through space in star tetrahedrons? Disappearing through solid objects? What would Dr. Hearty say?

"If the stars were the doorway *in*," Tara blurted out, chewing on a half-eaten chocolate bar, "then where's the exit?"

"I haven't thought that far ahead, Tara," huffed Dillon, still admiring the circular room. "But Henry must have wanted someone to find his laboratory, otherwise he wouldn't have left the note."

"I agree," said Kipper, looking at everyone. "Seems old man Fickle wanted someone smart to find it," Kipper patted himself on the back. "Like *us*."

"Exactly," said Dillon with a smile. "Adults wouldn't care—they'd probably destroy it."

A cool breeze entered the room. Tara stood close to her brother, while Tommy backed into Kipper. Their frightened faces were enough for Dillon to know what they were thinking. They finally had a taste of what he'd been feeling since the day he moved there.

Dillon strode over to the laboratory table. A print of Leonardo da Vinci's man canon captured his interest. It wasn't the print that intrigued him, but the fact that someone had superimposed a thin vellum over it. Dillon moved closer to get a better look.

Drawn with a fine pencil was a two-dimensional star tetrahedron, a circle, and a square!

The top apex of the star was about an inch above the man's head, and the same below his feet. The circle touched both apexes. The square was centered and the four corners exceeded about an inch past the circle. A thick line ran through the center. Dillon somehow knew the line represented the fluorescent tube.

Below the image, written in scribbled writing were the following words:

(π) Phi ratio=1.618 (rounded to three decimal points)
This magical number is found in the star tetrahedral field
that encompasses each human body. It's capable of
traveling into other dimensions or realms of existence.
The tube enables us to breathe life-force energy.

Dillon nearly fell backward. Now he knew why he kept seeing the circle, and later, the square. The circle flashed golden and the square turned violet. Dillon blinked and the colors vanished. "I found the answer to my assignment!" he whispered, archiving the image. Dillon's conscious mind was unable to grasp its full meaning. But somewhere, in the deepest regions of his being, he knew an explanation was stored.

He wasn't at all perplexed about the two-dimensional drawing. What fascinated him was how the drawing was brought to life. How had Henry Fickle built the miniature star tetrahedron? Where were his blueprints? And how had he activated the human-sized one around his body? This was a mystery even Dillon couldn't answer. Dillon had been given a gift: he was allowed a glimpse inside the complex mind of this brilliant man.

Suddenly, more scribbled writing appeared on the vellum. Intrigued, Dillon leaned closer and read:

> Our bodies are the measuring stick for the universe.
> All of life, including the earth and the moon are contained
> in geometrical proportions within us. We were never
> separate from anything, but a part of the whole.
> If we attempt to separate from nature, and each
> other, there will always be conflict.

Dillon stared intently at the words. He felt something spark inside. His total essence, including the atoms, were the same as the stars . . . the trees . . . the ocean . . . everything! He stood in awe. He wondered if anyone else knew this knowledge.

Moments later, the words vanished.

Leonardo's man canon was far more intricate than Dillon had perceived. He had seen the drawing at various times, but had never given it a second thought. A profound insight struck him. If the star vehicle could penetrate other realms of consciousness, then the words in his head must also come from the same place. The unlimited cosmic universe! Just as when an inventor thinks of an idea, most likely someone from another part of the world is thinking of the same one. Whoever gets to the patent office first, wins!

The others didn't seem to notice Leonardo's drawing or Dillon's new finding. Tommy was standing by wooden shelves, peering into glass jars, laughing. Tara amused herself with the bubbles floating around the room. And Sarina was talking to Kipper over by the circular bookcase.

Dillon saw a beaker spit a glob of puke on Tara's white shirt. She didn't even notice. He wondered. Would his friends even be interested in his discovery? "We all have our own interests," a unfamiliar voice inside replied.

Dillon decided to keep it to himself. He felt terribly alone and began to understand Fickle's long years of isolation.

Dillon pondered again: Some aspects of being psychic were no different than being an inventor like Fickle or an artist like Leonardo.

It was a personal experience that only the psychic person could appreciate. It didn't matter, after all, what others might think. What was important was what the person thought of themselves.

Dillon focused his attention on a bunch of wall charts and motioned everyone over. He saw Kipper and Tommy cringe. The charts must have reminded them of school, which was only a week away.

One displayed the periodic table and included diagrams of atoms, protons, neutrons, and electrons. Another displayed human anatomy, including the brain. A few were on astronomy and another on geometrical shapes and mathematical formulas and calculations.

"Help!" screamed Tara, struggling to free herself. "Let go!"

They all held their stomachs in laughter.

Tara had backed into a full-size skeleton wearing a white lab coat. Embroidered on the left pocket, in emerald thread, were the letters: H. F.—A mechanical pencil, ballpoint pen, and scientific calculator sat in the pocket.

"Check out the initials," said Kipper, reaching forward to touch the material.

Tommy and Sarina stepped forward, while Tara stepped back. She seemed uncomfortable standing next to a pile of bones.

Dillon wasn't interested. He wandered over to the bookshelf. "That's interesting." He pushed up his glasses until they set clearly over his big eyes. "According to Ralph Picit, *after* Fickle received the large package of books, he mysteriously vanished. But I don't see the titles here."

Kipper came striding over.

"That's odd," shrugged Kipper, looking over at Dillon. "They should be here with the others."

After viewing book after book, they came to the conclusion that the strange books were missing, and according to Kipper's watch, it was very late.

"How do we get home?" asked Tara in despair.

They started banging on the walls, hoping to find the star tetrahedrons to transport them back to the attic. Panicked and tired, they searched frantically for a way out.

But no door was found.

Tommy kicked a pencil that was lying on the floor and said aloud, "Why is there a way in but no way out? There has to be an exit!"

Meanwhile, Sarina was looking up at the picture over the desk. It was a profile of an older man. He had thinning gray hair and a scruffy beard. He was sitting at a desk holding something, while pointing to it with his other hand.

The others noticed and drifted over.

"What are you looking at, Sarina," said Tara in a curious tone, walking toward her.

"Jumping catfish!" cried Kipper, clearing away the cobwebs. "It's old man Fickle! I'd recognize that wrinkly old face anywhere! Check out his beady eyes!"

"That's him all right," said Tommy, standing alongside Kipper. "What's that screwball doing?"

Dillon shifted in closer, squinted, and said, "He's holding something. Let me see, it's . . . a . . . *scroll!*"

By the distant look on Dillon's face, you could tell his mind was churning. He lowered his eyes. "That's it!" he shouted, looking up. He reached up and kissed Fickle's picture. "The man's brilliant! He's trying to tell us something!"

Tommy shot Dillon a weird look, and then he said, "How could he tell us something when he isn't even here."

"I'll prove it to you," Dillon insisted, standing in front of Fickle's desk. "Everyone look at the picture, and then look here." He pointed to the wooden desk. "Now, what do you see?"

Fickle's desk, with its deep scratch in the right leg, resembled the one in the picture. Even though Fickle wasn't there himself, he was giving them subtle hints. Dillon knew the picture was an important clue.

He didn't waste any time searching through the drawers, sifting through hundreds of papers. He was determined to find the scroll, however long it took.

He abruptly closed a drawer. "I don't see it anywhere!" He kicked another drawer shut, knocking over a pencil cup. Pencils rolled off the desk, spilling onto the floor.

"Gee, Dillon," laughed Tommy. "Your as neurotic as Fickle. And I thought I had a temper."

Dillon ignored Tommy's comment.

"Don't worry, Dillon," said Sarina in a soft voice. "Maybe Mr. Fickle doesn't want just anyone to find it." She beamed at Fickle's picture. "He looks like a smart man. Don't you think so?"

An idea traveled through Dillon's head like a surge of electricity speeding through a wire. "Thank you, Sarina," he muttered, staring at the desk. "Sorry, everyone. Guess I got carried away." Dillon lowered his head, then looked up. "But Henry's no fool. He'd never leave something important out in the open. Would *you?*"

Everyone but Tommy shook their head. He seemed uninterested in finding a stupid roll of paper. Dillon sensed he was up to something, but by the time an image appeared—

CRASH!

It was too late.

"Look out!" yelled Dillon, attempting to break Tara's fall.

Tara had lost her balance. Hundreds of papers went sailing in slow motion. The image that had popped into Dillon's inner eye was Tommy pushing his sister.

Luckily, Tara hadn't hurt herself, but looked rip-roaring mad. As she turned to face her good-for-nothing brother, Kipper grabbed her arm.

"Look, you guys!"

Tara must have landed on a secret button, because a long rectangular compartment slid out from Fickle's desk.

They gaped open-eyed at each other.

Afraid of a trap, and with one eye closed, Dillon slowly slid open the cover . . .

Before his wide eyes was the ancient scroll.

CHAPTER TEN

THE ENCHANTING BLACK BOX

The scroll looked richer than Dillon had anticipated. He held it close as though it were a priceless document. The parchment was thin as onion skin and secured with a triangle-shaped seal. Instantly, Dillon saw the silver-cloaked stranger in his mind's eye. *The opening of the seal,* the man had said. Dillon sat in the chair and placed the long scroll in front of him.

The opening of the seal!

The others bent closer. Dillon swallowed hard and then gently pulled. The seal broke in half, and the scroll was free. Drawn across the parchment was a sword with an emerald-green star embedded in its handle.

Dillon gulped. He recalled his vision. This was the sword that murdered Henry Fickle! The sword had plagued his dreams and scared him in the bathtub. The oddest thing about it was it always looked so real—and now it had come to life!

Dillon jolted backward against the chair as the sword slashed and ripped the parchment. The precious document was torn to pieces before his wide eyes. The sword disintegrated suddenly into dust and disappeared.

Dillon's heart sank horribly. What just happened? Was the scroll cursed? Would he have bad luck for the rest of his life? He shouldn't have opened it, he thought.

"Now what do we do?" asked Kipper in disbelief. "We'll never know what was inside."

"Well, that's that," said Tommy flatly, staring at the clump of fragments.

The girls stood in silence, looking at each other.

Dillon's heart was in pieces like the scroll. It was unreadable! That wicked sword destroyed the ancient scroll, he thought angrily. He had trouble speaking. "I didn't mean to—"

"*Look!*" cried Tara rapturously, pointing to the desk top.

The others stood at a safe distance with their mouths hanging open. From the remnants of death, the pieces came together and restored themselves—a new scroll was born.

Before Dillon could reach out, the scroll unrolled across the desk. The parchment was blank. It looked as though it were waiting for its author.

Then something startling happened.

A swarm of emerald-green letters appeared out of thin air and hovered above the scroll. The letters dangled like musical notes, then pasted themselves down. Drawn across the parchment was a triangle-shaped seal with the words "The Seal Is Opened."

A slight breeze lifted Dillon's hair. He sensed someone in the room and quickly spun around.

Two very tall people, dressed in full ancient Egyptian garb, were standing behind them.

The kids let out piercing screams.

Kipper recognized the figures at once—but it wasn't possible! Standing before his startled eyes were the Egyptian god Thoth and the goddess Isis—the stone statues guarding Fickle's house.

A strong fragrance filled the air. Dillon had never smelled anything like it. It calmed his nerves and lifted his spirit. He glanced at the others. They too looked relaxed.

The goddess gracefully stepped forward with her headdress and wide, sheltering wings. She smiled widely and in a soft voice said, "I speak your language. I am Isis, goddess of the underworld, who brings life to the dead. It's time for the records to be passed to a new generation of children—children who desire peace above all else. I am mother of the healing waters and give you my blessings." Isis dipped her finger in a small vial she was holding. She rubbed the fragrant substance in the sign of the cross over each of their foreheads. When she was finished, she stepped back.

They stood in silence.

The male god with an ibis, or heron-like bird, on his head stepped forward. He was holding a papyrus roll and stylus. He also spoke their language. "I am Thoth, god of the moon and keeper of the holy records. I have for you a message. Only the one who reads with an open mind will be given the keys."

Dillon had difficulty hiding his joy. He was afraid to blink for fear of missing something. His head exploded with questions. *What* keys?

Thoth stepped closer. In a deep-but-gentle voice he said, "It's the young who will lead the world. Laughter and innocence shall bring thy people back. So is it written in the stars. Remember this day, and prepare for the synchronistic events to take place." Thoth stepped back. "Behold!"

Without warning, an intense force of thunder shook the room, crashing a row of glass bottles to the floor. The girls clapped their hands to their mouths as lightning ripped the sky.

The townsfolk and local sky watchers saw something entirely different. A greenish glow appeared in the heavens and formed an arc of light. It started to shimmer and dance with a cluster of stars. In all the years he'd been there, McNulty had never witnessed an aurora borealis. It just wasn't common in Willow Creek, until tonight. Harriet Wimple swore she saw an apparition—the head of a short stork and huge wings. She gave her head a shake and looked again. But they were gone.

The lights in the laboratory blinked off. When they came back on, Thoth and Isis had vanished, and the seal and the words with them.

The short meeting with the Egyptians made a profound impression on Dillon. He'd been blessed by two of the oldest gods in recorded history! Although the parchment was blank, Dillon sensed something stirring.

They huddled excitedly, looking over Dillon's shoulder, anticipating the moment.

"Why's it taking so long?" grumbled Tommy, pacing behind the others.

"Shhh!" hissed Tara. "You can't rush things like this!"

"Hey," said Kipper abruptly, gazing at the blank page, "something's happening."

As though an invisible pen were writing upon it, fancy emerald-green words appeared. Dillon leaned forward and read:

It's written that the seal has been opened! This is a time of great celebration and rejoicing. Let he who found this scroll be congratulated. Bravo! You found my picture—good. It tells me you're piecing solutions together with your brain and using that remarkable mind, which I'm pleased to say is an unlimited resource. You've been wondering how to leave this room. I'll give you a small hint: the exit is behind the desk.

The words mysteriously vanished.

Dillon stared at the scroll in confusion, while the others whispered to each other. How did the scroll *know* about them finding Fickle's picture? Or about their conversation on finding the exit? Was someone listening? Either the scroll had intelligence or *the walls had ears.*

Dillon stood up and turned to Kipper. "The scroll says the exit is behind this desk," he said, placing his hands on one end. "Let's give a tug, Kipper, shall we?"

The others took a step back. They were all expecting to see a secret door, but—

"That's silly," chuckled Tara. "There's nothing there."

"I don't understand," snapped Kipper, while scratching his head. "The scroll clearly states the way out is behind *this* desk." He slapped his hand hard to the surface.

Dillon was still thinking.

Suddenly, they heard a sweet voice floating through the room.

"The scroll didn't say that, Kipper," said Sarina timidly, standing behind him. "It didn't say it was precisely *that* desk."

For a young girl, Sarina was smart and observant, although the boys couldn't admit it.

Dillon wheeled around and stared deep into her eyes. "I guess it would be too logical, Sarina. No, I think good old Henry's playing with words."

"Playing with *what?*" asked Tommy gruffly. "Will you *please* talk in English. Besides, there's no other desk here."

"Oh, yes there is," Dillon chuckled, looking up at Fickle's picture. Everyone stood beside him looking utterly bewildered.

"*Look!*" he said, pointing to the picture. "Voila! There's a desk." Dillon reached up, snatched Fickle's picture from the wall, and laid it on the floor.

A blue button was recessed flat to the wall. Heart pounding, Dillon plopped himself down on the chair, not wanting to lose his concentration.

"What are you doing?" said Tommy, trying to figure him out. "What about this button?"

"I'm waiting for the scroll to tell me," he whispered, ignoring Tommy's frustrated face.

Tommy Flick rolled his eyes.

Dillon was in a world of his own as the rest hung excitedly over his shoulder. A new inscription appeared with the same emerald writing. He buried his nose in the scroll and read:

You found the blue exit button—wonderful. Press this button, but I repeat, only when you're ready. I might add, the stars were a fascinating entry, but not too practical. It's undeniably difficult, especially having nosy mothers peering around every corner; however, never fear, my dear friends, I've discovered a bright solution.

Dillon realized in a roundabout way that the scroll meant *his* nosy mother. But how did it know that Dillon was the reader? He read:

In the compartment where you found the scroll, you'll see a black box with four buttons. At the top is a large orange triangle for entering my laboratory. When you press it, make sure nobody's watching, because you'll disappear from wherever you are.

Dillon felt like he was in a toy store with the hottest toy. Did the scroll say *disappear?* Was it really possible or just a silly fantasy? Dillon lowered his head, fixed his sliding glasses over his long nose, and read:

Below the triangle is a green circle and a five-sided, purple pentagon. At the bottom is a golden square. A word of warning: The other buttons are forbidden until further notice. Now get the box.

"*Forbidden?*" Tommy asked bitterly. "Why can't we touch them?"

Kipper shrugged. "He must have his reasons."

Dillon turned to Kipper. "How can the box be in the same compartment the scroll was in? There was nothing else there."

"Right. There was only room for the scroll."

"This is getting weirder and weirder," said Tara, standing with her hands on her hips.

Dillon stood up and looked at the compartment. The cover was closed, but he remembered he'd left it open. Or had he? He shrugged, then slid it open. Just as the scroll proclaimed, a small black box was lying inside.

Their rational brains had trouble accepting such things, but their minds welcomed the experience with delight.

"It's magic!" cried Sarina gleefully.

"I reckon old man Fickle's a bit of a magician," agreed Kipper.

The compact box fit perfectly in the palm of Dillon's hand. He ran his fingers around the smooth edges. His blue eyes glinted behind his glasses at the four colored buttons. He'd never seen anything like them. None of the shimmering colors was ever likely to be in an artist's pallet, a paint store, or the biggest box of crayons. They were indeed not of this world!

The box was made from a foreign material. It looked alive, pulsating shades of gray. Dillon's fingers hovered over the buttons and hesitated. He changed his mind, quickly stuffing the box in his pocket. He sat back down and waited.

"This is ridiculous, standing over an old scroll!" Tommy shouted furiously. "I think it's some kind of trick! I don't believe it at all! You're all wasting your time!" Tommy started walking away. "That stupid box is probably a fake, anyway!"

Tommy's sudden anger went right through Dillon. It was like Tommy had popped his balloon. Dillon's heart told him they weren't being deceived. His short-tempered friend was gravely wrong, he thought.

Even Kipper was surprised by Tommy's harsh behavior. "What's the matter with you, Flick? I never saw you act like this before."

"Leave it to my brother to ruin things," groaned Tara, throwing her hands in the air.

Tommy ignored them.

"Why don't you believe Mr. Fickle, Tommy?" asked Sarina gently. "I think he's telling the truth. Aren't you the least bit interested in the magic box?"

Although Sarina's voice seemed to calm his temper, Tommy wasn't giving in. He pretended to take interest in something slimy floating in a jar.

"Forget him, Dillon," said Kipper, shaking his head.

More emerald ink appeared over the blank page. Everyone except Tommy huddled over Dillon's shoulder. Silently, they read:

Before we begin, put aside all judgment and outdated beliefs; they'll not serve you here. Don't allow your doubting or rational brains to interfere with what I'm about to share with you. Use your own intuition, it'll guide you to the truth. Forget how you perceived the world to be and what you've heard from others. There's much more to life than you think.

Your Friend,
Henry Fickle

Once again, the words vanished, and the page was wiped clean. Everyone looked at each other, and then turned toward Tommy. Their excited faces must have told him he was missing something good, because he nonchalantly strolled over.

Dillon noticed more writing and quickly elbowed Kipper.

They read in silence, while Tommy loomed over Kipper's shoulder. There was only one problem. Tommy couldn't see a thing. The page was blank. Tommy knew something was there because everyone's eyes rolled from side to side and their lips mouthed the invisible words. He huffed away in silence.

Started all it how. Wait! Stop! Rewind! How it all started . . . yes, that's much better.

My dear mother died when I was born. Later, my father remarried, and I was raised by my wicked stepmother until I was about your age. She'd randomly create rules, and living at our house on Windy Drive became unbearable. After my father's untimely death, I inherited the house and half his money. My stepmother had gotten the other half. Soon after, she left town with a hefty pocketbook. I never heard from her again.

The page went blank. Dillon sensed additional writing coming any minute . . .

The fancy writing continued:

Uncle Berk, who was my father's only brother, agreed to stay at the house until I finished school. He took no money, except for food and expenses to maintain the house. Uncle Berk was easy to get along with and pretty much left me to myself. I loved reading. After school, I'd spend hours at the public library, rummaging through thousands of books. You might say I was curious, like yourselves. I had quite a few questions that needed answering.

Dillon admired Henry, relating to his passion for books. He wished Henry could see *his* book collection. Maybe Henry would be proud of him. Although his mother wasn't wicked, she still nagged him sometimes. Dillon continued reading:

At night, I'd spend endless hours in the garage, brainstorming new ideas. But the noise and unexpected explosions caused folks to talk. Uncle Berk encouraged me to continue and would often say, "Carry on, Henry. You're going to be a famous inventor someday, you'll see." One day, I noticed odd things happening. Objects moved as I focused my attention on them. Light bulbs popped when I entered a room, and things I had predicted came true—things I couldn't have possibly known before. I was different from other kids, but in those days—well, it wasn't accepted. I was unprepared for the cruel and hurtful remarks that would affect me so deeply.

Dillon stopped reading and glanced up at the others. They had the same expression on their faces. *Explosions . . .* objects *moving . . .* light bulbs *popping . . . predictions?*

Dillon was bursting with joy. This was the second person he knew who was like *him*. The more he read, the more he realized how much he'd in common with Fickle. He too wanted to become an inventor and do great things. Henry Fickle would be Dillon's incentive. Dillon continued:

I was known as the weird kid, teased by my classmates. Teachers kept me after school for predicting future exams, and the town thought I was working with the devil. I had no friends except Uncle Berk. I lived like a hermit, lonely and terrified. I was convinced I had lost my mind. I just wanted to be normal like other kids. I had no one to turn to, until I met Lady Norton.

The page went blank. They stopped reading, whispering quickly to each other. Dillon knew that wise old woman was holding hidden knowledge.

Dillon saw Kipper's eyes wander. Dillon tuned in and heard Kipper's thoughts. His friend wanted to learn how to predict answers for school tests. If he sold them, he'd be a millionaire! Dillon grinned. Lady Norton's face flashed in his mind's eye. *If you misuse your gift for selfish purposes, it can be taken away,* she had said.

They bent forward when new words arrived and read:

When I was your age, Lady Norton looked the same, just like you see her now. She's been able to preserve her older look, which she fancies, for 461 years. She explained that what I was experiencing was referred to as a sixth sense, or psychic ability. This made sense, because I often found religious beliefs and school teachings too limiting. I had been plagued with questions and was forced to search in a different direction. I knew I was missing a large piece of the puzzle. Before Lady Norton would agree to help, I had to erase from my mind the belief systems that had deluded, restricted, and held me back from experiencing my true purpose. Only then would I be able to open and expand my mind. In short, I had to believe in myself and trust that my experiences were training me for what was yet to come.

"Four hundred and sixty-one?" Tara said in awe. "Who would have guessed?"

"I wonder what's her secret?" said Kipper aloud to himself. "I could make a fortune . . ."

"Why would anyone want to live that long anyways?" said Tommy, overhearing their conversation. "And old to begin with. Why wouldn't she want to look like twenty?"

Sarina and Tara nodded.

But Dillon didn't hear their conversation. He was lost in his own mind, trying to absorb everything. It was like Fickle and he had led parallel lives. They'd experienced similar things, especially psychic things. Dillon recalled *knowing* who was on the phone before anyone answered it. More than anything, Dillon wished Fickle were alive. He longed to tell him he understood how he felt and that he wasn't alone anymore.

Henry Fickle's ancient scroll had exceeded their expectations. They'd no idea such things were possible. It was clear Lady Norton and Henry Fickle were much more than they had thought. The fancy writing continued:

Lady Norton would say, "Life has many mysteries, Henry. If you want answers, go no further than yourself."

Years later, I graduated from high school and Uncle Berk left town as agreed. I lived alone and wrote to Uncle Berk about my progress. Occasionally, I'd travel, studying eastern philosophy. I worked a short time at a research company. As a matter of fact, I had many inventions that could have solved a great many of the world's environmental problems, but the company turned them down. I became depressed and went to Lady Norton with my issues. She said my ideas were too advanced. "The world's not ready for you yet, Henry. Don't pay any mind, people are filled with greed. Just keep inventing!"

Dillon frowned. He felt sorry for Henry. Why would someone

reject his brilliant inventions, especially if they helped the planet? Those people were either insanely stupid or afraid they'd lose *money*. Dillon thought of them as the biggest "#$%@#*s" in the world. Yes, that would be a better name for them. He read on:

I resigned my position with the company and dedicated my life to my work. I would no longer waste time or associate with people who were ignorant of what was happening to this planet. In my small garage, I would persevere through any obstacles, including the human-made word called "failure." I would not accept the word "failure" in my vocabulary. When I had a tough day and my inventions weren't working, I'd start over the next day, refreshed and confident that a solution was forthcoming. If I tried a hundred solutions, the odds of one of them working were excellent. And work they did!

One fateful day, when I was vacationing in Peru, my garage (laboratory at the time) was vandalized. ALL my records were either confiscated or destroyed. My equipment was smashed and my dreams shattered. I would have to start over. From then on, I kept things secret, securing my laboratory exactly where you're standing. After dark, Lady Norton and I would meet privately here. The unusual books that you heard of weren't attainable through the library, so Lady Norton suggested a few mail-order sources. I know you have many questions, but you must learn patience—everything happens at just the right time.

In conclusion, the ancient scroll was given to me for safekeeping. I was to guard it with my life. But in order to do that, I had to make some changes. From my alchemical skills, I was able to make the scroll imperishable and resistant to all elements. I blended a bit of magic, if I say so myself!

Remember the orange triangle will transport you to the laboratory. The blue button behind my picture is the exit. That's all you need to know for now.

Best regards,

Henry Fickle

P.S. So you don't get in trouble, and if you don't mind, I reorganized the time back to seven-thirty!

The emerald-green writing was complete. It was as if the author had retired the pen. Kipper looked down at his watch. It read seven-thirty.

Dillon's face glowed. He went to reach for the scroll, but it rolled itself up, flew to its compartment, and disappeared into the depths of Fickle's desk.

Tommy couldn't see what was written, but he'd heard Kipper repeat the last part. "How could Fickle alter time?" asked Tommy, looking unconvinced. "It's impossible."

"Is it really?" Dillon said, swiveling around to Tommy. "Kipper's watch tells another story. I believe there's many things we don't know, and probably never will. The ancient scroll represents a doorway in, and I'm stepping forward—with or without you!" Then he turned his back.

"Who cares about the time, Tommy," said Tara, giving him the evil eye. "You should be grateful, but no, you *always* have to complain about something."

Tara continued to rant and rave. She didn't notice Tommy cup his hands like a pair of earmuffs, blocking out her voice. It's not that Tommy didn't want to believe—his mind was holding him back. Besides, magical things lived in fiction and in the movies, not in the real world.

How very wrong Tommy Flick was.

"It seems weird," said Kipper, staring at the picture. "It seems old man Fickle's here. And the spooky part is, he knows it's *us*."

Kipper did have a point. How did the scroll or Fickle know it was them? How could it detect what they were thinking and doing? Everyone looked around the room. Tara clung close to Sarina's side, almost smothering her.

"Henry Fickle! If you're really here, show yourself!" demanded Dillon. Then he backed against the wall, standing close to the others. "I call you forth!"

The only sound they heard were bubbles coming from the beakers. The room went cold, covering their arms with goosebumps. Again something invisible brushed past them.

By the time Dillon's last words had traveled through space, the lights flickered into darkness. They couldn't get close enough and were soon stepping on each other's toes.

POP!

A loud noise broke the deadly silence.

Panicking, they heard movement in the room. The lights flickered on. Standing quietly by the laboratory table was the silver-cloaked man.

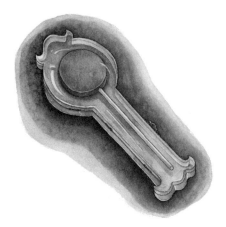

EVERCOOL FICKLE POPS

E veryone was stunned, except Dillon and Sarina. They recognized the white-bearded man with the unusual clothes and mighty sword.

Fear washed over Dillon as he closed his eyes. He remembered the silver-cloaked man holding Fickle's package and a sword. The man's guilty, Dillon thought. After all, he had his vision as proof.

But what bothered Dillon the most was that he couldn't see more. The video in his mind had suddenly stopped. The more he tried to rewind or fast-forward the scene, the more scrambled it looked.

For a few horrible seconds, they weren't sure whether to run or bow down to the man. They cowered against the wall, realizing they'd lost their voices. How had the stranger entered the laboratory without a star tetrahedron? Or the black box?

"I have been waiting for your invitation! It's about time you called!" said the man in a deep voice.

They looked up into his bright face. His light eyes looked almost white. They were relieved to see his mouth crinkled in a smile, all except Dillon. He didn't trust the man.

"Er, sir," mumbled Kipper. "Do you know what happened to Henry Fickle? He vanished from Willow Creek a year ago."

Dillon wanted to cover his friend's mouth, but wasn't fast enough.

Was he nuts to speak to this stranger? The man's dangerous, Dillon thought. He wanted to tell the others. But he'd have to reveal his vision, which would expose his abilities. What if they didn't understand? What if they didn't like him anymore? He'd lose his only friends. Dillon remained quiet.

They continued to stare at the stranger, but nobody else dared to speak. A slight grin broke across the man's face as he took a few steps forward. His long cloak swept the floor.

"Don't worry, I mean no harm," the man said at once, picking up on their discomfort. "Come, I want to show you something."

The others inched slowly forward, while Dillon hesitated behind, thinking. This was it. The stranger had them cornered. Any minute, the man would take the sword out. They'd all be killed! He'd no choice; he'd risk telling his friends. The man's deep voice startled him.

"Gather round, gather round!" said the man. "I have a delightful surprise for you."

"Wait!" Dillon shouted, turning pale. "Don't go—it's a trap!"

The others looked bewildered by Dillon's odd behavior, but their curiosity won them over.

"It's true!"

"Geez, Dillon," said Kipper with a grin. "Now you sound like Tommy."

The man smiled, and then turned his back and faced the laboratory. The others moved to his right side. They watched him crank a brown knob. Several beakers began churning and mixing.

Dillon heard giggles and chuckles. It sounded like children at the playground. The soothing sound of laughter seemed to break the tension. *Where's the sword?* Dillon edged carefully forward.

Nobody said a thing as the man busied himself. He cranked a blue knob, then scrambled to the other end. His cloak dragged along.

Dillon heard banging from a stainless steel freezer. A high-pitched noise sounded like something was trying to get out. Dillon's imagination ran amuck. The stranger wasn't going to kill them with the sword, he thought. Instead, he'd set loose tiny creatures that would eat them alive.

The man turned, smiled at Dillon, then turned back to the steel box. He yanked down a red handle and waited a few seconds until the banging subsided. He shifted the handle back up. No sound came from the freezer. Everyone took a step backward as the stranger opened the door.

Dillon cringed.

A white cloud escaped, and lying there were six colored objects. Everyone except Dillon leaned in for a closer view.

The man reached in and took the objects in his large hands. A last breath of mist drifted off their surface. "Ah, yes!" said the man, gleaming down at the shiny treats. "They're now edible. Aren't they wonderful?"

Finally, as nobody seemed to want to talk, Sarina said, "They look like lollipops."

The man laughed long and hard. His long beard swayed back and forth. It appeared Sarina's innocent-but-keen observation pleased him.

Dillon's mind raced. "*Lollipops?*" he whispered. "What's going on?"

"Go on now," said the man brightly, placing a purple one in his mouth. "Don't be shy." He bent over. "There's one for each of you." His lips puckered.

Sarina looked excitedly at Dillon for approval, but he shook his head firmly.

The man couldn't fool him, he thought. The appealing treats were deadly. Yes, it would be much easier to poison them—there'd be no struggle. But Dillon was baffled when the stranger placed one in *his* mouth. Before Dillon could stop her, Sarina took a bright orange one, then happily sucked away.

Dillon watched in horror. "I told you not to take one," he whispered to her sternly. Any moment now his little sister would start gasping for breath. Dillon waited . . . and waited . . .

But nothing happened.

Dillon's sister appeared content, still licking away. Dillon couldn't stand it any longer. He was dying to try one. "What do you call them?" He chose a red one. "I never saw anything like them." Dillon looked at it carefully, then stuck it in his mouth. His lips puckered when he tasted a burst of red flavors. The taste was so incredible, he couldn't put a name to it. With each lick, it tasted like something different.

"Evercool Fickle Pops," said the man proudly. "It's my latest invention and healthy for you, too. There's no additives, preservatives, or artificial colors. You can suck on them for one week, and they'll never shrink. But on the seventh day, after midnight, they'll disintegrate." He suddenly took the purple pop from his mouth. "Ah! A new flavor—a snazzberrie!"

Tara and Sarina giggled.

The man put it back in his mouth and continued. "I'm still working out some minor details. It so happens your tongue goes numb for a few days after sucking on the green ones." His face looked confused but then reassuring. "But don't fret, eventually the feeling comes back."

"Cool!" Kipper grabbed a blue pop from the man's large hands. "Sir, does Charlie's Candy Store sell them? You know, after the week's up, how do we buy more?"

"Ah, I'm afraid they're not for sale. They're my most secret and private invention. But I do suspect when the week's up, you'll have had enough of them."

Tara had finally found something that lasted more then ten seconds. Where could you buy a lollipop with a world of flavors? She lunged forward, snatched a yellow one, and sucked through pursed lips.

Only a green pop remained. Tommy slouched, sulking, at the last one. Then his expression changed to anger in a matter of seconds.

"Hold on! You stole that invention from Henry Fickle! You even used his last name!"

Everyone looked quickly at Tommy. He had to go and open his big mouth again. But Tommy was right. The man never revealed his name. In fact, he hadn't even answered Kipper's question about Henry Fickle—he seemed to have avoided it altogether.

For some reason, Dillon was just beginning to feel comfortable with the guy. But he couldn't help but wonder. Had the stranger stolen Fickle's package and his invention, then murdered him? But Dillon's heart lightened when he realized that he didn't have to tell his friends after all—they suddenly had their own suspicions.

Many questions filled their heads. Now they wanted the truth. Who was this man, and why was he messing with Fickle's laboratory? The man seemed to read their suspicious looks.

"Calm down, young fellow!" chuckled the stranger. "Time due in all. STOP! Rewind. All in due time. Yes, that's better. I suppose you're entitled to the truth."

The man took a deep breath. They gasped when the stranger suddenly eyed them. His gleeful eyes made them nervous. Was he the type of man who smiled just before killing? Had Fickle been an unfortunate case who placed his trust in this stranger?

Dillon saw Tara sucking hard on her yellow pop, then gaze longingly at it. Dillon tuned in to her thoughts. Tara was afraid the man would take the pops back because her pain-in-the-butt brother had insulted him!

Dillon caught a glimpse of the massive sword, thinking he was right. They were doomed. He suddenly tasted an unbelievable flavor from his red pop. Got to have it, he thought. He quickly scanned for the secret ingredients, hoping to make his very own pops—if he made it out alive.

The man raised his right hand and snapped his large fingers. Dillon crouched low, thinking it was the end.

Instead, something remarkable happened.

A transparent figure stepped out of the silver-cloaked man. The new, pasty figure stood silently to the left of the stranger.

Everyone froze at the ghostly sight of Henry Fickle!

Fickle's lifeless body stood hunched over. His yellowish, beady eyes glared darkly at them. His beard was mangled and his shirt stained. He looked weak, scrawny, and sickly—nothing like the tall, vibrant stranger.

With their Fickle Pops stuck to the insides of their mouths, their voices were lost in a silent scream. Sarina's face looked as pale as Fickle's, and Tara started frantically scratching her arm.

The stranger snapped his fingers again. Fickle's withered body was gone, but the strange man remained before their puzzled eyes. What was going on?

SNAP!

Fickle's faint and ghostly body reappeared. The air was full of questions.

Dillon glanced over at the others. Instantly, he was bombarded with their fears and thoughts. Kipper wondered, what magician's trick was this? Tommy was thinking not only was his *mind* failing, but his eyes, too. Sarina feared being taken away to some distant place. But Tara's mind was quiet—she'd sunk into a stupor with her mouth open. There was no doubt. Henry Fickle was dead.

Fickle and the stranger turned to each other, smiled, then turned back toward the wide-eyed group.

Dillon's glasses fell down his nose. Did the two men know each other?

The stranger looked to Fickle, then to their frightened faces. "I feel you're ready for the truth," the man said finally, glancing at Fickle's silent figure, who was nodding. Dillon noticed Fickle was missing quite a few teeth.

"About a year ago, I received a large package in the mail. I had been waiting anxiously for it to arrive. I was hoping it contained the missing links to my research," said the man.

Dillon's eyes widened. The stranger was talking about *the* package—the one he'd stolen from Fickle. But why was the stranger talking like it was *his*?

"One night, after decoding information from the package, I found my answer. My answer happened to be intertwined in quite a few sources. The missing pieces fit together perfectly. It made so much sense that I'd asked myself why I hadn't seen it years ago. I suppose when the student is ready, the teacher arrives."

The stranger smiled widely and then continued. "My body was old. In order to continue my work, I needed a new one. After receiving enlightenment and viewing my body as light, I was able to ascend and disappear from this dimension. I passed effortlessly through the void, totally conscious, and then reappeared in the higher realms of spirit. There was no need to go through the death process. That's why my body hasn't been found—I took it with me! Shortly after, I reconstructed my body. Three days later (Earth time), I chose to return in a vibrantly healthy one." The stranger placed his hand to his chest, as if pleased with his choice.

The five stunned kids listened, not knowing how to file this updated information, not knowing what to think, or if they were ever going to leave the laboratory. Fickle's pearly-white body kept eyeing them. He was making them even more nervous than they were before.

"I'm the soul of Henry Fickle. Henry Fickle and I are one.

Someday you'll understand. But for now, you must believe, I wasn't *murdered*." He glanced over at Dillon and grinned. "Because of the grid being in place and rapid vibrational changes, many of us have ascended. Not everyone is ready for this knowledge, nor would they believe it. Nevertheless it's true. After all, I experienced it myself."

The ghostly body of Fickle faded until it disappeared. Only his wrinkly face remained, which was now transposed over the stranger's face. It smiled wickedly and popped out of sight.

Dillon's curiosity was overwhelming. Who would have guessed the silver-cloaked man was Henry Fickle! Dillon felt relieved Henry was alive and wasn't murdered. It would explain Dillon's scattered vision—he wasn't able to see the whole video. Dillon scanned Fickle's body. He definitely liked the new one. At least it wasn't as scary looking as the old one.

After taking a few deep breaths, Dillon said, "Sir, I mean, Mr. Fickle. May I ask you a few questions?" Dillon felt weird addressing the man as Henry Fickle, but knew it would take time for the initial shock to wear off.

Henry Fickle nodded. "Please, call me Henry."

The new Henry seemed much more patient, not like the old prune some of them had remembered. It wasn't proper to call him "old man Fickle" anymore. He was no longer old.

Everyone listened to Dillon's line of questions.

"Can you tell us what was in the package?"

"Ah, the question I've been waiting for. The package contained books and ancient documents. Let's just say, from my world travels, I'd met wonderful friends." Fickle's eyes sparkled. "There were books on Atlantis, which, by the way, did exist. There were books on time travel, but the others . . ." Fickle drifted for a moment, staring at the walls. "I had access to Leonardo da Vinci's sketches, ratios, inventions, calculations, and drawings; Egyptian hieroglyphics; and records on ancient civilizations, including the Sumerians. Within these sources, I'd arrived at my answer. My research was complete!"

Dillon immediately thought of the star tetrahedrons and Leonardo's drawing. "Does the star . . . you know . . . the ones we traveled in . . . were they part of your research?"

Fickle's smile widened. "Smart boy. I must say, you're on the right track. Someday, when you're ready . . . now is there another question?"

"At the town hall, you mentioned the 'opening of the seal.' I saw the triangle-shaped seal in your scroll. Can you elaborate on this?"

A hush fell over the room as Fickle stroked his long beard and then heaved himself onto the laboratory table. They were turned toward him, listening with rapt attention. A glob of yellow puke erupted from the beaker and spit on the front of Tommy's shirt.

"Yuk!"

"I'll tell you what you should know at this time. I only speak the truth, but I know what each of you is capable of comprehending. You're the chosen ones, who found my laboratory and my precious scroll. You willingly solved the puzzles and the riddles." Fickle stared down into their innocent eyes. "You were curious to learn about my sudden disappearance and open-minded enough to learn the truth without judgment." His eyes flashed toward Tommy.

Dillon thought whatever was meant about the *chosen ones* seemed to be important. A sudden idea came to him. Could it be that Fickle had hoped their specific group of five would find his laboratory? Dillon started to speak, but Fickle continued talking.

"The scroll is now camouflaged to outsiders. Once you've broken the seal, only *you* can see its true contents. If anyone else finds it, it'll only show trivial matters."

Dillon had a sudden vision of battling intruders who came to steal the scroll. He saw himself defending and guarding it with his life. Then he saw the most horrid face laughing at him, galloping away on horseback. In a thunderous night storm, the dark figure had tricked him and stolen the old document. It was too late. The scroll was gone forever. Could this have been the same dark warrior from his dream? Dillon broke out in a sweat.

"You activated the scroll, which was an awakening and introduction," Fickle said, smiling down at them. His eyes lingered on Dillon, who nervously tried to forget his vision.

"The scroll has been given to you, if you're willing to accept it. I must say, it won't be easy. When you complete the scroll's message, you will have mastered an honored code." He leapt from the table with a deafening thump.

Dillon's mouth watered when he thought of being at many places at once. Playing tricks on his friends? The endless possibilities were beginning to sink into his brain. Maybe he'd leave one of his bodies at school while he took a vacation.

"If we take the offer, how do we let you know?" asked Kipper. "Do you have a cell phone?"

Fickle laughed. "I knew you'd ask that question, Mr. Reeves."

"How'd you know—"

"If you accept this challenge, press the orange triangle button. Your acceptance will be recorded, and the scroll will be awaiting you on my desk. If you choose not to accept this path, the scroll will be moved to a distant place, the box will disintegrate, and my laboratory will self-destruct."

Fickle looked dreamily around. "My life's work is encoded in my soul—my laboratory has served me well. It has no use for me now. You have *three weeks* to arrive at a decision. The last day, after midnight, you'll not have a second chance."

The kids began to ponder the offer. Could they turn down an opportunity like this—to find out secrets about life and the universe?

Dillon thought it was his grand opportunity to step through the open door. It was scary and unknown, but if he turned Fickle down now, how would he ever know the truth? Dillon heard a babble of chatter in his inner ear. With the will of his mind, he fine-tuned the dial—the thoughts became audible.

Dillon clearly heard his friend's voices. Tommy didn't want people to think he was chicken. The girls had mixed feelings, but didn't want to be left out. And Kipper thought about mastering the art of disappearing. He was definitely taking the offer.

Dillon smiled. He kept thinking about the synchronistic events. It was no coincidence his family moved to Willow Creek—it was his destiny!

Fickle interrupted their thoughts and said, "You don't have to decide at this very moment. Go home and think about it. So before we part, do you have any questions?" His eyes wandered back to Dillon.

"You're leaving us?" said Sarina at once, glancing sideways at Tara. "Are you coming back? Will we see you again?" Her eyes began to well with tears.

Fickle recognized the disappointment on their faces, but said, "I'm afraid not. I have been waiting for you to call, but understood you all have free will. We'll see each other someday." Fickle paced across the room. "You have no idea the impact you could have to change this world for the better. You'll see—and you'll always have my blessings." Again, Fickle peered at Dillon like he was anticipating more of his questions.

But Dillon was still thinking. How could a handful of kids possibly change the world? It would take more than that, he thought.

Dillon finally looked at Fickle. He wanted to ask about the afternoon duel and mention his troubling dreams, but he didn't have much time. What he said instead was, "Could you tell me about the sword I saw in my bathtub . . . and the one under your cloak?" He stared at the opening between the large green buttons.

Without giving Fickle a chance to reply, Dillon blurted out the rest of the questions that surfaced in his mouth. "What about the sword in the scroll? Can you tell me how you can be at so many places at once? I heard what happened at the town hall. And one last question, would I be able to take a book home? I'd really appreciate reading one." Dillon took a deep breath, absorbing oxygen into his lungs. He could finally rest.

From the looks on his friends' faces, they'd no idea what he was talking about.

Fickle unhooked a few of his bottom buttons and parted his cloak, revealing his long massive sword. The emerald star illuminated before their interested eyes.

Tommy and Kipper exchanged excited looks.

Fickle looked bemusedly at them before speaking. "This sword and the bubbly one I created in your bathtub represents a past time. I hope I didn't scare you, Mr. Allbright," he said. His eyes narrowed.

Dillon shook his head. He didn't want to admit he was scared to death. All the same, he knew he couldn't hide his fear.

"I'm afraid you won't understand what the sword represents unless you continue with the scroll. The answers are all there. When you uncover the truth, you'll know the sword and its history. That's all that can be said for now," said Fickle firmly, fastening his cloak buttons.

The kids knew not to press the issue.

Dillon wondered. *Past time?* This question continued to stir in his head.

"Oh, about my being in many places at once," Fickle said, while looking around the room. "I'll give you a brief example."

Fickle snapped his fingers three times and around the room stood three Henry Fickles. They were talking at the same time, but doing different things.

One was carrying on about the weather, while another was sharpening his blade. The other was trying to pull a thread off his cloak. The original Fickle was grinning at the confused-but-excited faces.

Fickle snapped his fingers again. The other Fickles vanished. Good old Henry had a strange way of displaying the truth, otherwise who would believe it? He looked as childish and excited as the wide-eyed bunch. And seemed proud to show them things they'd never seen before.

"I can split my essence many times and not be reduced or contracted, which means I can be many places at once," explained Fickle. "Ah, belief is the prerequisite to the keys."

The face of Thoth appeared in Dillon's inner eye. *Only the one who reads with an open mind will be given the keys.*

Everyone stood there, listening intently. Fickle looked dreamily around the room.

"Believe in what's not seen, and *know* it's forthcoming. If you count on your eyes to tell you, you'll be deceived. They have a way of distorting the information. Funny the way people think the lenses of their eyes show the true picture, isn't it?"

Dillon's head lowered. He had prejudged his vision of Fickle, without knowing the whole story. He believed his eyes were correct, but had forgotten to ask his heart the truth. Dillon vowed to never make that mistake again.

The time they spent in the laboratory had proven what they didn't know. The knowledge they had grown up with was a small fraction of life's many mysteries.

Dillon drifted off. Could it be that Fickle had touched on an ancient wisdom? A lost code? And if he had, was it perhaps an honor to delve deep into his world?

This was a lot of information to absorb. This once-in-a-lifetime offer was on the table. It was like signing a contract for a lifetime guaranty of free information. They paid not by money, but by determination, dedication, and willingness to learn. The results, however, were unlimited.

The meeting came to an end as Fickle's smile faded. "Whatever decision you make, I'll not judge you. I must go. Nevertheless, children, I'm omnipresent—that means I never leave you." Fickle made a sudden turn to Tommy. "Oh, Mr. Flick, I do think it wise to expand your mind, otherwise you'll be left behind. Blank parchment is for people who choose not to believe." Fickle's eyes narrowed.

Tommy nodded, his ears turning a shade of pink.

"Yes, well, until we meet again, my dear friends," said Fickle, bowing. "I bid you farewell."

He placed his purple Fickle Pop into his mouth and with one swish of his silver cloak, faded from view. But his essence stayed with them.

CHAPTER TWELVE

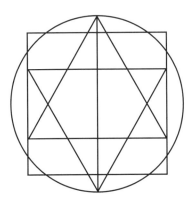

THE BLUE EXIT BUTTON

It took quite some time for them all to move in front of the blue exit button. They weren't sure what Fickle had devised, but assumed it was something spectacular.

"What was Fickle talking about before?" Kipper asked Tommy. "A *blank* parchment?"

Tommy shrugged.

Dillon looked over at Tommy, but Tommy avoided his eyes. It had occurred to Dillon that Tommy hadn't been quite truthful. But then, he thought, as he recalled his earlier experiences of being psychic, belief can't be taught . . . no, one must discover it alone.

Lady Norton's screechy voice spoke suddenly in his head.

"You're quite right, dear. You see, belief is a de-energized emotion, living inside our hearts, waiting for love to ignite it. I'm afraid Mr. Flick's heart would have to open, but only when he was ready." Her voice faded away. "—believe and the magic will follow—"

Dillon smiled and then had a sudden disappointing thought. "Henry forgot to show us where the new books are," he grumbled. His heart sank as he slumped over.

"What's *that*?" Kipper asked Dillon, looking up at the pointed ceiling.

They all watched a paper fall like a leaf, making its way to the

* 97 *

floor. Dillon reached up and snatched it.

"Something important, Dillon?" asked Kipper anxiously.

But Dillon couldn't speak; he was contemplating something. A grin slowly formed over his face. It got wider and wider. Dillon scrambled over to the circular bookcase, lowered his head, shifted his right sneaker over a few inches, and stamped down.

Tommy's eyes rolled, while the others had to stifle their laughs. It wasn't long before their smiles were wiped clean from their faces.

The books fell into the wall, and different books slid forward.

"What's going on?" asked Tommy, looking uncertain.

Dillon happily explained. "Fickle dropped us a clue. This paper is a drawing of *that*," he said, pointing to the bookcase.

"But why did you stamp your foot?" asked Tara, looking quite impressed.

Dillon's face was flushed. "Do you see this red *X* engraved on this specific floorboard? You know what they say, '*X* marks the spot.'"

Sarina admired Dillon's intellect but figured he must have help. After all, her brother had seen and heard spirits—spirits that were knowledgeable in every conceivable field. Dillon must have many mentors.

On the shelves were the books from Fickle's package, plus many more. Dillon would be doing a lot of reading that year.

"C'mon, let's go!" said Dillon, taking a book. He felt nervous and excited as he approached Fickle's picture. He reached forward and pressed the blue button.

They closed their eyes and waited . . . and waited.

"What's going on?" said Tommy irritably. "I knew Fickle—"

A screechy noise inside the wall muzzled Tommy's words. It sounded like rusty gears grinding and churning. The clanking became louder as it moved closer.

Dillon fixed his wide eyes on the wall. Was something going to burst out and swallow him whole? His imagination wrestled with mechanical beasts, distorted creatures, and evil monsters.

Suddenly, the wall opened, and a giant slide appeared.

Dillon took Sarina's hand. "Let's go!" he cried, as he held a book called *Sacred Geometries of Life* tightly to his chest. A star tetrahedron happened to be on the front cover. They jumped onto the slide, not knowing where it would take them, and disappeared inside the dark wall. "Hold on-n-n-n—"

Only the echo of Dillon's voice remained.

The others leapt forward.

They tumbled and bumped against the wide slide and each other. Kipper's large sneakers banged against Tommy's head, while Tara helplessly slid backward. Their screams faded as they plunged ever deeper into the darkness.

The speedy slide dipped downward through a maze of twists and turns. The air smelled of dampness as Dillon caught glimpses of leaky pipes and flourishing mold.

Unknown to them, the wall sealed itself. Fickle's picture snapped back into place, covering up the blue button. The important books traded places with the boring books, and the lights switched off. It was all very strange, as though the room was tidying up.

After hurling over a steep section, Dillon and Sarina plopped down in a pile of hay. They moved just in time, as a jumble of bodies landed beside them. Directly in front of them was an arched doorway. The weird thing about it was it had no doorknob.

"Where are we?" whispered Sarina, covered in hay.

"Awesome!" cried Kipper, glancing up. "Faster than a roller coaster! I want to go again!"

Dillon laughed. He knew Kipper'd be talking about it for days.

"Fickle sure had us this time," smirked Tommy, nudging Kipper in the arm. "I thought he was catapulting us to our graves." He laughed at his own humor.

"Look at Tara!" bellowed Kipper. "Her *hair!*"

Tara's curly head of hair was intertwined with hay. Her shirt was stained with chocolate, and she had a yellow tongue. Tara rubbed her stomach. It seemed the speed of the slide made her queasy.

A short time ago, everyone had placed their Fickle Pops in their pockets. Now they realized it would be difficult unsticking them.

Dillon wondered why Fickle didn't invent a special case. He felt in his other pocket. He'd been concerned that with all the bumping, the small box would break. So he was pleased to know Fickle used not-of-this-world material, which make for an unbeatable product. The box was still intact.

Kipper went to open the door, but it was impossible. "What's going on—where's the handle?"

Tommy pushed his way forward. "I'll take care of it," he said confidently, flexing his bicep. Tommy threw his weight into the door until his face was red with effort.

But the door wouldn't budge.

"Now what do we do?" asked Tara anxiously, staring at the closed door.

"Any ideas, Dillon?" asked Kipper nonchalantly. "You know . . . can you *see* . . . I mean . . . think of anything?" He glanced quickly at the others, then changed the subject. "We have confidence in you, Dillon. If anyone can find a way out, it's you!" Kipper looked wide-eyed at the others, who were nodding their heads.

Dillon began to wonder why everyone was suddenly interested in him? Something was going on. Even Tommy looked at him encouragingly. Dillon was ready to say something, when Sarina opened her mouth to speak.

"Maybe we have to say the magic word."

Those few inspirational words triggered a familiar scene in Dillon's inner eye. Although he hadn't quite finished reading *Bed-Knob and Broomstick,* he owned the classic Walt Disney movie version. It was one of his favorite movies. He must have seen it a hundred times.

A memorable scene from the movie appeared. Miss Price was tidying up the magic bed with Cary; Paul was watching and Charles was sulking. He didn't believe the bed could be made to fly by turning a simple bed-knob and giving it instructions where to go. Miss Price sang Charles a song. It was about the age of not believing.

Suddenly, the vivid scene faded. Dillon saw Henry Fickle and all five kids standing in front of the arched door. Fickle sang a song. He kept repeating the same verse. As soon as they all joined in, the door clicked open, and the image disappeared.

After a few moments, Dillon said, "I know this sounds stupid, but it's worth a try. I hear . . . I mean . . . I know this song . . . well, it's important we sing it together."

The looks on their bright faces confused Dillon. They didn't even think his idea was silly. Even Tommy didn't protest. Finally Dillon said, "Forget it. Just follow my lead. Okay?"

They all nodded enthusiastically.

Dillon stood before the arched door and sang Fickle's verse:

"Frazzle dazzle—stop your moping—if you believe, I will open!"

The door wriggled.

Dillon's heart jolted with excitement. He encouraged them to join in. They sang together:

"Frazzle dazzle—stop your moping—if you believe, I will open!"

The door shivered and shook.

This time, they threw their hearts into it. They sang aloud:

"Frazzle dazzle—stop your moping—if you believe, I will open!"

Dillon heard a series of clicks, and the door slowly opened.

Everyone cheered together.

They crowded around Dillon, taking turns giving him a pat on the back. The heat rushed to Dillon's face as he stood thinking. Once in a while, a song comes along at just the right time. In order for the door to open, they all had to believe. Dillon thanked Fickle privately.

Kipper peered into the darkened room, which looked deserted. Of course, they argued over who would be first. They flipped fingers and Tommy lost.

After everyone passed over the threshold, the doorway suddenly vanished.

It was all very odd. There were no seams to indicate a door was even there. The dark room held no sign of anything recognizable, until Dillon bumped into a solid object. "It's Dad's workbench! Fickle dropped us in my parents' basement!"

Sarina and Tara cheered together. "We're home!" Then they hugged each other.

Suddenly, the lights went on. Everyone went quiet. They heard Mrs. Allbright's voice from the stop of the stairs, which made it sound twice as loud.

"DILLON! ARE YOU DOWN THERE?"

"Be right there, Mom!"

They heard the door close, and her steps dying away. Gradually, a babble of talk broke out.

"You're all right, Dillon," said Tommy.

But Dillon didn't hear. He stood, staring at where the doorway had been. He thought about Fickle's laboratory. What adventures were waiting for them in the scroll?

Something moved in his pocket. Dillon gasped. He slowly lowered his hand inside. Everyone noticed and huddled around. Was it a thousand-legged spider? Or something worse?

When Dillon retrieved the dreaded thing, he was holding a small fancy case. His red, Evercool Fickle Pop rested inside. Fickle must have read his mind, he thought. "Thank you, Henry," he whispered to himself.

A deep voice instantly filled his head. "You're welcome, my dear boy. Enjoy!"

Dillon was pleased to see the others had their very own cases. Sir Duke caught his attention as he fluttered past the windows. Dillon grinned. He strongly suspected Lady Norton was going to get an earful that night.

Kipper threw an arm around Dillon's shoulder and took him aside. "Glad you moved to Willow Creek, Dillon." Kipper's face suddenly looked serious. "We're best friends, right?"

"Of course, why?"

Kipper leaned in and whispered, "If we're best friends, you don't have to be afraid to tell me you're psychic." Kipper punched his arm. "I think it's cool."

Dillon's face burned. How did Kipper know? It was Sarina, he thought bitterly. He'd seen her speaking with Kipper by the circular bookcase. Then Kipper must have told the others. Dillon turned, and saw everyone standing behind them, staring.

"Oh, please don't be mad, Dillon," said Sarina at once. Her eyes welled with tears. "I just knew they'd understand. They like Miss Norton and Mr. Fickle—I thought they'd like you, too."

"I think it's wonderful, Dillon," said Tara enviously. "I mean, you're lucky."

Kipper nodded in agreement.

"Listen, Dillon," said Tommy. "I have to admit, you're weird sometimes . . . you know . . . kissing Fickle's picture." Tommy laughed. "But we could use a good psychic around. School tests?" Tommy nudged him. "You know what I mean?"

Dillon blushed. This wasn't what he'd expected. They were

nothing like the people he knew before. For the first time, people were interested in *him*. He felt like a celebrity. They asked all kinds of questions and begged for private readings. Dillon was more than happy to tell the others about their future with great detail.

" . . . you're going to have a confrontation with a kid wearing a black tee shirt . . . the last name starts with the letter *B* . . . it will turn out in your favor," he told Kipper.

"Who is it?" Kipper asked.

"Dunno. Sometimes, I just get parts of names or symbols."

Tommy edged his way in front of Tara to ask Dillon a question.

"It's my turn, Tommy!" huffed Tara, shoving her brother. "Move over!"

"Stop pushing, Tara!"

Dillon drifted off. There are some trustworthy friends who can share your deepest secrets and they'll always remain your friend. They happen to live in a small town called Willow Creek.

Dillon told them everything: his invitation, his light body, and flying with Sir Duke. Sarina and Tara's eyes bulged throughout his story. Tommy looked envious. And when Dillon told them what Lady Norton had said about his gift, Kipper grabbed his arm.

"So what do you think your gift is for?"

Dillon shrugged, while walking toward the steps. "I'm not sure, but Lady Norton had said—what was it?—'your gift, you'll know what to do when the time comes.'"

"You'll figure it out," said Kipper, looking quite honored to walk beside him.

Everyone started talking at once. And together they walked up the narrow steps.

But unknown to Dillon, at this very moment, Lady Norton and Henry Fickle were clicking their tea cups and saying in hushed voices, "To Dillon Allbright—the boy who will change the world!"

If you love this book, we invite you to send us your comments, ideas, drawings and fan letters to Dillon, Sarina, Lady Norton, Henry Fickle and all the others to:

The Sorcerer's Press
119 Mertz Road
Mertztown, PA 19539

Include your first and last name and age so we can include them if we publish any of what you send us in another book. Please also enclose a letter from your mom or dad saying it's okay for us to use what you're sending in the book.

For the last ten years, James Browne has been creating images that catch the eye and touch the heart of viewers of all ages. Taking reality and fantasy and molding them together, he's able to create a world of its own, where imagination soars. James is the illustrator of such titles as "The Amazing Snail" and "Into Enchanted Woods." His works continue to be displayed and sold throughout the world. He maintains his studio and residence in Phoenixville, Pennsylvania with his inspirational wife, Nadine.

"I have a lifetime to paint, with a subject matter that is endless, with one goal in mind, and that is, to keep the child in all of us."

—J.B.

To see the imaginary world of
award-winning artist/illustrator *James Browne*
visit his web site: www.jamesbrowne.net

ORDER COPIES FOR
FRIENDS AND FAMILY

Check Your Local Bookstore or Order Here

YES, I want *Henry Fickle and the Secret Laboratory!*
Please send me _____ copies at $18.00 each,
plus $4.00 shipping & handling for one book,
and $2.00 for each additional book.
(*PA residents only must include 6% sales tax*)

Mail this order form with
check or money order payable to:

The Sorcerer's Press
119 Mertz Road
Mertztown, PA 19539

Name: _____

Address: _____

City: _____ State: ____ Zip: _____

Telephone: _____

(In case we have any questions about your order)

THANK YOU FOR YOUR GENEROUS ORDER!